Kids @ the Crossroads

Crusades

by Laura Scandiffio
art by John Mantha

annick press   toronto + new york + vancouver

NOTE TO READERS

While today we call the campaigns of the medieval knights in the Holy Land
Crusades, the people of the Middle Ages did not. The word *crusader* (from an
expression meaning "marked by the cross") was used only in later centuries.
At the time they called themselves *pilgrims* or *cross-bearers*. The Muslims who
occupied the contested lands called the European invaders *Franks*.

About Me

Name:
Hans. This is me.
Age:
12 years
Home:
Wiesdorf (a German village that's a speck in the <u>dukedom of Westphalia</u>, which is a patch in the Holy Roman Empire). This is my house.

Future job:
Same as my father, a <u>wheelwright</u>
Pet:
We can't afford to feed an animal we're not going to eat, but we do have a pig we're fattening.
Brothers and sisters:
Otto, 19; Gisela, 8
Things I can do:
Hit a moving target with a sling (but not as well as Otto). Catch our pig when he gets loose. Carve toys out of wood for Gisela. Play the flute, a little. Build a fire.

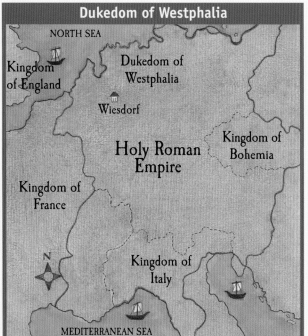

Dukedom of Westphalia

NORTH SEA

Kingdom of England

Dukedom of Westphalia

Wiesdorf

Holy Roman Empire

Kingdom of Bohemia

Kingdom of France

N

Kingdom of Italy

MEDITERRANEAN SEA

Wheelwright

A Fine and Useful Trade

The village wheelwright builds and mends wheels for anything a horse or man can pull—wagon or carriage or dung cart. He's very picky when choosing his timber, then he chops a hub into shape with an ax. The blacksmith (who always helps a wheelwright) drives on the red-hot iron bands, then plunges it all into cold water to shrink the bands tight (and stands back from the hissing steam). Next, the oak spokes are pounded with a hammer into the spots the wheelwright has marked and stuck into the curved rim.

It's a trade to be proud of, and better than working a lord's lands, as the peasants do. Still, there are other trades that make you more important in town—a goldsmith, for instance, or even a wool weaver. Each trade has its own special club, called the guild. The guild makes sure everybody's work is good enough, decides how much to charge and what wages to pay, helps its members, and keeps an eye on competition. Some boys learn a trade with their father, but others leave home when they're young to become a master's apprentice (and get to see a bit of the world). You might even travel around, working here and there as a journeyman, before you're ready to make your own masterwork—the best example of your work you can show—and bring it to the guild. If they give you the nod, you're a master yourself!

THE RULES

Take the dried anklebones of a sheep—you'll need at least two. The bones have four sides, all different (one flat, one curved in, one curved out, one sinewy), and each is worth less or more. Toss the bones in the air and catch them on the back of your hand, or you can let them fall on the ground as long as all the players agree before you start. Add up your points and see who wins.

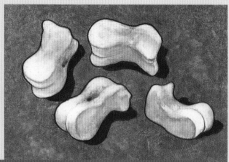

Parzival and the Grail

Things I'd like to do:
Ride a horse instead of walking everywhere. Travel, especially on a ship. Train a falcon. Meet a knight.

Things I love:
The bread my mother bakes. The smell of fresh wood shavings in the workshop. The glow of the forge and clang of the anvil at Ulrich the blacksmith's (my father's friend).

Things I don't love:
Sitting crouched over my workbench when the sun is shining or my belly is empty. The wool tunic that belonged to my brother Otto, and which I'll have to wear until I grow out of it. Too itchy! Cabbage soup (which we eat when there's no meat—too often).

Favorite song:
"Welcome, Oh Wanderer." Because the wanderer has been everywhere and can answer all the riddles. (That's the kind of song I like: a ballad that tells a good story or asks a riddle. No love laments for courtly ladies, thank you, or songs that teach a lesson.)

Favorite game:
Knucklebones (I'm getting too old for leapfrog and hopscotch.) Father calls it a foolish boy's game, but Ulrich plays it sometimes—I've seen him.

Favorite story:
"Parzival and the Grail." Because he becomes a knight even though his mother and everyone else try to stop him.

17th day of June, 1212

An Unexpected Guest

Something strange happened last night. I'm still not sure what it all means.

A sudden noise woke me up. A voice, I thought, but whose? In the cot next to mine, my sister didn't move a muscle. (She sleeps through anything.) I listened in the dark. Again I heard it: a stranger's deep voice, in the next room. We don't get many visitors in our village.

I snuck out of bed and tiptoed toward the door. It was cold! It's been spring for ages, but our house stays icy till my mother lights the fire in the morning.

For a moment I lost my nerve: I could just picture my father frowning at me for being out of bed. (He lost his temper with me twice yesterday for dawdling and daydreaming.)

With a gentle push, I opened the door a crack. I spotted a glow from his workshop. And I heard voices again. A crackling noise told me my mother had lit the kindling. I peeked into the room.

My father was hunched over the long wooden table where we eat. His back was turned to me, so I felt sure he hadn't seen me. Across the table, a man in a traveler's cloak sat facing him. I noticed that my father's tools were lying here and there. That was odd! He always stows them away so neatly at night.

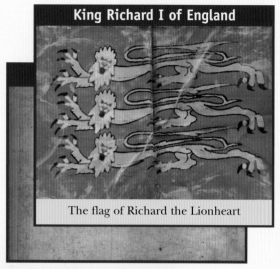

King Richard I of England

The flag of Richard the Lionheart

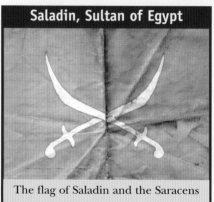

Saladin, Sultan of Egypt

The flag of Saladin and the Saracens

I slipped next to my mother and pretended to yawn when she glanced at me. But I kept my eye on the stranger. He was hard to see in the dim light, but his dark eyes shone and his bearded face was broad. He was gulping from one of our cups, and wiped his beard on his sleeve.

"We've heard no news of such a venture here," I heard my father say. He talked in the dry voice he uses to discourage conversation from a customer he doesn't like. Why didn't he like this man?

The stranger didn't seem to notice. "Do not doubt it," he answered. "There's been a new call for able men to <u>take up the cross</u>." (That made my spine tingle! I knew what he was talking about. At the same time, a familiar face flashed brightly in my mind. But I bit my lip and listened.)

The stranger started to tell my father about traveling preachers who were going from town to town, recruiting men. "For the battle against the heretics," he said.

The face I'd remembered—my brother's face—seemed to flicker and fade. It's been two years since Otto left, and I find it hard to picture him clearly for longer than an instant. His image slipped away, and I had to blink hard against the tears that sprang from nowhere into my eyes.

At this point my father coughed and muttered, "These things do not concern a simple tradesman." Just like him! All he cares about are his wheels and his workshop. Why wasn't he asking this man if he knew anything about Otto? For months now, he and my mother have stopped even saying his name. Doesn't he care anymore? But then, I did notice a tremble in his voice. Maybe he and I were thinking about the same things.

I stopped sneaking glances and looked boldly at the stranger. He pulled his cloak tight around himself and leaned forward. "Tradesman, farmer, or knight: many say it is every Christian's duty to rid the Church of her enemies—wherever they may be."

Now I was confused. Wasn't the whole point to win back the Holy Land? What other enemies were there?

"What about Jerusalem?" I blurted out without thinking. They turned their eyes toward me, and I felt my face get hot. But I wanted to know.

The visitor smiled at me, but the smile didn't reach his eyes.

Take up the Cross

THE FIGHT FOR THE HOLY LAND

The year is 1212 and campaigns to the Holy Land have been under way for more than a hundred years. The Christian world is divided into two parts: the western one in Europe, and the eastern,

known as *Byzantium.* In 1095, Pope Urban II, the religious leader of all Christians of the West, called upon the knights and rulers to liberate the Christians of the East from Muslim rule. Alexius, the emperor of Byzantium, had asked him for help because his empire was in danger of being surrounded and conquered by armies of Turkish Muslims. The ultimate goal of the Christian armies is to control Jerusalem, the city sacred to Christians, Jews, and Muslims alike. Christians who "take up the cross" and fight for Jerusalem are promised forgiveness for their sins. What's happened so far:

1099	The Christians capture Jerusalem and found their own states in the Holy Land. (Their victory becomes infamous among Muslims for the brutal treatment of the city's defeated people.)
1148–49	A second campaign is launched to counter new Muslim conquests.
1187	Saladin, Sultan of Egypt, takes back Jerusalem. Pope Gregory VII proclaims a third campaign.
1189–92	King Richard I of England, known as the Lionheart, captures Cyprus and Acre, but not Jerusalem. The battles end in a peace treaty.
1201–5	A fourth campaign to recover Jerusalem is a disaster: the Christian army gets mixed up in Venice's wars and ends up sacking Constantinople, a city it was supposed to protect.
1209	Another campaign begins, in Europe. This time it's against heretics in the south of France known as Cathars, or Albigensians. Their ideas contradict what the Church teaches.
1210	The ruler of *Outremer* (as the Christian states in the Holy Land are known) appeals for help: his truce with the Muslims is about to end and he wants to be ready for war.

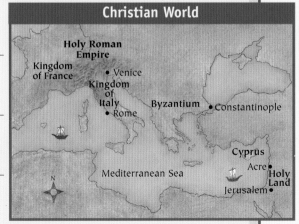

Christian World

Holy Roman Empire
Kingdom of France
Kingdom of Italy
Venice
Rome
Byzantium
Constantinople
Cyprus
Acre
Holy Land
Mediterranean Sea
Jerusalem
N

"There are enemies within and without, boy," he said. "This particular nest of wasps is dug in deep in the south of France. As for the Holy Land, some say the days of a Christian kingdom there are numbered."

Now my mother spoke up. "Of course, our son is much too young to take note of such things." In the glow of the hearth I could see her brow was creased, and she stared hard at my father.

The visitor nodded. "It's knights and fighting men who are wanted, not babies and women." (My face got hot again, and I was glad it was too dark for them to see it turn red.)

What the stranger said next took me by surprise. "Sometimes these <u>preachers</u> get more than they ask for. They stir up the common folk and then can't stop them. I've heard of a boy from Cologne, a real troublemaker—"

My father coughed loudly, and the stranger shot a glance at me. He shook his head and drank again. I shifted from foot to foot, wondering if he would go on.

He set the cup down and smacked his lips. "From the River Seine to the Rhine," he said at last, "it seems young people everywhere are gripped with the same madness—a kind of spring fever, I suppose."

Madness? Fever? I wanted to ask him more, but my father nodded at me. "To your bed, now." I noticed he avoided my eyes.

Afterward, I stretched out on the cot I used to share with Otto and felt my heart beating fast. If he were still here, I could talk to him about all this, like we used to. When he first left, I used to imagine him on his way to Jerusalem with the other young men. He might be on a dusty road in Italy, or aboard a ship (while I was left here to fetch and carry and never see anything new). Months went by, then a year. He must be there now, I would think, holding the sword Ulrich made for him once he decided to go, just like that. Even though Mother cried and Father raged at him.

I thought over what the stranger had said about the Kingdom of Jerusalem's numbered days. What did he mean? What would happen to the men who'd gone there? I tried to eavesdrop in the dark, but the murmurs were too quiet.

Suddenly it was clear to me. I'm not the little boy I was when Otto left—I'm already 12. (Hasn't my mother told me, with that sad look, how much I look like Otto now that I'm older?) What if I follow where he's gone? Others have. Maybe somewhere people are taking

Preachers

How to Recruit Fighters for Our Noble Cause

A HELPFUL SCRIPT, BY ABBOT MARTIN OF ALSACE

Traveling preachers, when you summon men to fight in the Holy Land, always make these points:

✝ Our Christian brothers and sisters in the East are in danger and suffering as we speak.

✝ Just as a vassal defends his lord's lands, so we, all vassals of Christ, must come to His defense when places holy to Him are under attack. (Preachers: Bring along pictures of Christ suffering during His earthly life to make your point clear.)

✝ Men, the world leads you into sin, but you don't have to put away your swords, give up a life of action, and enter a monastery to earn eternal life. You can fight in the Holy Land to earn forgiveness for sins.

✝ Any women and young boys listening: you might get ideas about joining. The answer is no—the weak must serve His cause in other ways.

✝ The French preacher Bernard of Clairvaux used words like

these to fire up the crowd! He once got such a flood of volunteers that, when he ran out of crosses to hand out to those who took the vow, he tore up his monk's robe into strips. Of course, it didn't hurt to have the French king at his side wearing the cross himself.

✝ Read my speech for more ideas. (I not only preached the cause, but joined it myself!)

"Today Christ addresses you in His words through my mouth. Christ has been expelled from His holy place—His seat of power … The Holy Land, which Christ impressed with His footprints, in which He cured the lame, caused the blind to see, cleansed lepers, raised the dead—that land, I say—has been given over into the hands of the impious …"

to the road right now. I could find Otto myself and fight alongside him, and once we succeeded, we could come home together.

Now my idea won't leave me. It's all I think about. I know I can't tell Father or Mother or even Gisela about this. No one can know.

21st day of June, 1212
Kings' Bones and a Troublemaker

Everything has changed so quickly that I don't know where to begin. I'll try to tell it all just as I remember. Maybe then it will make sense.

First of all, a lucky chance came sooner than I expected. My father announced that he was traveling on St. John's Day to the Cologne fair. He needed a fine drawknife and cloth for my mother, and I hardly heard what else. My heart jumped—Cologne, the city the stranger talked about, where that so-called troublemaker is! (I'd heard more rumors about him—Nicholas is his name—but more of that later.)

As for our nighttime visitor, I prodded Father with questions, but I didn't get much from him. Here's what I did find out: The stranger is a mercenary! Off to fight for money in the army of a great French lord. He had knocked on our door when he saw our wheelwright's sign. When my father saw the cross on his tunic, he felt bound to give him food and shelter. I guess I looked too eager to hear more, because after that Father snapped shut like a clam.

I begged Father to take me to Cologne, promising I would help, and to my surprise he agreed. He was in a foul mood, though—he grumbled that if he's to feed so many mouths, one might as well be useful. My mother made me promise to stay away from ruffians. (While chopping wood in our yard the other day, I overheard a village woman sobbing in our house, and I'm sure I heard her say her son had disappeared in the night. Mother's kept a close eye on me ever since.)

We left before dawn in Ulrich's cart. I should have been excited, but to tell the truth I was sore and cross. Gisela had tossed and snored so much in the night that I had hardly slept at all. And my stomach was growling—just watery soup at supper, and not

The Cologne Fair

A Herald's Message of Welcome, from the Merchant Guild

Why journey all the way to the fairs of Champagne when a mere day's journey from many villages and towns will bring you to this important crossroads, where the River Rhine, bringing ships from far and wide, crosses the land route from Saxony to Flanders. Farmers and simple tradesmen, sell your cows, buy your wool here. Those of you with more to spend can afford the real luxuries: spices such as pepper (costly, but you can buy it by the peppercorn), saffron, and cinnamon from the Far East; mirrors from Venice; furs and skins from northern lands. Our city's own artisans weave cloth and fashion works of gold and ivory that are the envy of many foreigners. (They also love our iron, and use it to make fine armor.)

While you're here, don't be alarmed by all the strangers from foreign lands (and try not to stare).

You'll see English, French, Scandinavian, Flemish, and Lombard. Our merchants will be ready with our newest scales to weigh any coins in dispute (better than biting to check if they're genuine).

Enjoy the local ales and sausages and bread. (All fine and pure; the guilds see to that!) Watch the pageant with moving scenes from the life of Saint John.

A final word to the wise: Knights and ladies attending for pleasure, please keep a firm hold on your purse. Your fine clothes draw the cutpurses (surely not locals) like bees to a flower.

enough for a second bowl. But I forgot my hunger when we pulled into the city. What a difference from home! The roads in Cologne are wide and paved with smooth stones, not dirt. The timbered buildings are tall and rich-looking, and the riverside swarms with merchants and ships like bees in a hive.

I wonder how far those ships sail. To cities like Mainz on the Rhine, I know, but where else? When I try to picture places farther than that, I see only a haze, like a map with its edges worn away. I stared at the ships, and suddenly Wiesdorf seemed like a very small place.

The fair was grand and crowded. Only days ago I'd have been thrilled by it, but now I had something greater on my mind. After an hour of trailing Father through the market while he haggled, I wondered if I would ever have a moment alone to find Nicholas. Above the stalls I could see the cathedral's spire, and I remembered the stories I'd heard of the shrine inside. It's supposed to hold <u>sacred relics</u>—the bones of the Three Kings. I grabbed Father's sleeve and asked if I could go see it. He was frowning over a cloth merchant's wares. At first he just bobbed his head, telling me to meet him at the cart, but then he caught me by the arm. "Promise to be quick," he said. I nodded and fled.

WHAT EVERY PILGRIM SHOULD KNOW

There has been a sacred building near Cologne's city walls for a long time. The cathedral (the home church of a bishop) was built in the 800s on top of a church, which in turn covered a Roman temple. The archbishop housed relics in the cathedral, but the most exciting ones came here in 1164: the remains of the Three Kings, or Wise Men, who visited the infant Jesus.

Pilgrims come from far and wide to visit relics like the ones at Cologne. Many believe that very holy people (the saints), who acted for God during their lives here on Earth, are still able to help the living and plead for them in heaven. It's important to visit the actual ground where holy people walked, or to touch what's left of them (called relics), because these places and things are how the saints, now in heaven, stay connected to Earth. Some say the relics can heal the sick, too. Before you leave, you can buy a tin pilgrim's badge to sew onto your hat or hang from your staff. It proclaims that you've been here, and lets you keep the power of the saint's protection wherever you go.

A pilgrimage, when it's long and hard, is also a way to do penance for sins so you won't be punished for them in the afterlife. Some criminals are sentenced to a pilgrimage, and in the rare case of a very serious crime, the pilgrimage never ends. Such a wrongdoer wanders from shrine to shrine in chains, hoping that someday one of the saints will have pity and break his chains forever.

Of course, the greatest pilgrimage a Christian can make is to Jerusalem. Many believe that fighting in the Holy Land is really an armed pilgrimage. The pilgrim not only visits the holy sites but also goes to free them.

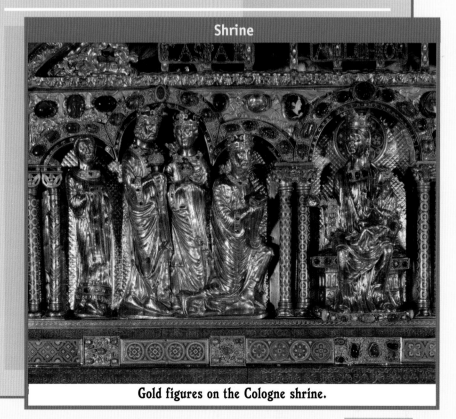

Gold figures on the Cologne shrine.

The cathedral is impossible to miss; it looms over the whole place like a big dark eagle over its nest. Pilgrims from all over come to see the holy relics inside—not only the chains that held Saint Peter, but something even more exciting: the bones of the Three Kings who visited the infant Jesus. People say the bones work miracles, curing the sick and all sorts of wonders. This was something I had to see for myself. I could already picture the look on Otto's face when I told him I'd been here!

I mounted the steps, past the sellers with their pilgrim's badges and ivory models of the church. The doors were open, and inside the daylight dimmed to a soft glow. My footsteps echoed as I walked up the nave. On either side, columns soared upward like giant oaks, and the aisle seemed to go on forever, like a path through an ancient forest. The air was as cool as the stones of the walls. Ahead I saw the altar in the middle of the building and, beyond that, high overhead, a chandelier fit for a giant's house, glowing with more candles than I could count.

At the shrine I felt a little disappointed. I didn't get to touch or even see the bones. They were inside a big golden box that looked like a cathedral itself. Then I felt stupid. What did I expect? The Kings lying there for just anyone to see?

As I turned away from the shrine, I heard shouts outside. I started retracing my steps down the nave.

"They're nothing but trouble!" It was a woman's voice, shrill.

"Well, I won't refuse them anything." A man's voice this time. "What if they are God's messengers—what will happen to us if we spurn them?"

Now I was very curious! I sprinted through the doors. Outside, boys of all ages were swarming before the stone steps. Some were ragged, but others were richly dressed. I saw apprentices in leather

Nicholas

WARNING! ALL CITIZENS OF COLOGNE AND FREEMEN LIVING IN THE PRINCIPATE OF HIS GRACE THE ARCHBISHOP

Be on guard for a boy of around 11 or 12 seen preaching in the city's public spaces. This boy, Nicholas by name, proclaims to have had a vision: that in the night sky he saw stars turn into a cross and heard a voice speak to him.

He wears an unusual cross stitched onto his shirt that looks like this, but our witness could not make out what it was made of:

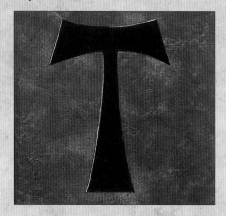

He is a fearless public speaker and has a way of attracting followers among the young and gullible. His intentions are unclear, but he seems to be rousing a mob to march to the Holy Land, where he claims their faith alone will bring triumph.

We, a group of concerned burghers, clergymen, and respected guild members, draw this dangerous matter to your attention. Parents: keep close watch on your children until this madness passes.

aprons and pages in bright uniforms. Girls stood here and there, too, some holding small children by the hand. One girl with wild tawny hair was stretched up on tiptoe, her eyes wide. She and everyone else stared in the same direction. A core of angry voices and pushing bodies was drawing everyone in like a whirlpool. Pilgrims from the shrine brushed past me to watch.

That's when I saw him. He was standing alone in the middle of the crowd. The others encircled him, but at a distance. He was tall and lanky, and his brown hair fell in messy locks around his face. On his shirt he wore a strange cross I'd never seen before. He didn't look any older than me. I'm not sure why, but I knew at once that this must be the troublemaker, <u>Nicholas</u>.

A merchant was shouting at him. "How can you expect to do what kings, dukes, and so many others have failed to do?"

"We'll obey God's command," he answered, "and carry whatever burden He places upon us." The children around him cheered.

It's not so much his words that have stayed in my head, but his voice. It's hard to describe. It sounded young, but it was ringing and strong. Without taking my eyes off him, I nudged my way through the crowd, trying to get closer.

Nicholas kept shouting over the din. "I am only the messenger, but I have heard a call so clear that it has swept all doubts from me. You and I—the young, the weak, the poor—have been called to end the struggle for God's holy city. He has put His trust in us, and we will not fail Him."

I've never heard any boy my age talk like that! Or any man, either. He wasn't arrogant, but he didn't sound afraid. Not at all.

A loud, sarcastic voice interrupted. "What will you use to fight the terrible armies of the Saracens?" It was a man in a stained butcher's apron. "Your pilgrim's staffs and songs?"

The answer amazed me. "We won't fight the Muslims. We'll save them. When they see the strength of our faith, they'll surely become Christians themselves."

The butcher started laughing. It made my blood boil, as if he'd laughed at *me*. But another tradesman told the butcher to hold his tongue. A monk cried out that this was all too rash, that without the blessing of the Church it was not meant to be. Shouts from others in the crowd drowned his voice.

I jostled hard to get past the ring of bodies around Nicholas, and slipped to the front. The next instant a stern voice fell like a hammer on my ears. "Stand back, there! Clear the way!"

How I hadn't spotted him before, I don't know. I must have been too thrilled by the boldness all around me. A man approached on horseback, wearing a bright tunic with gold braid. Bailiff or guard—whoever he was, he must have been important enough to scare people, because the crowd parted around him as he rode toward Nicholas. Before him, on foot, his young servant shoved anyone left in the way. I noticed the tawny-haired girl standing between the rider and Nicholas. The servant waved her aside, but she stood fastened to the spot, her eyes locked on Nicholas.

What followed happened very fast. I rushed to pull the girl out of the way. The rider's lackey whirled around, alarm on his face. Without warning, his arm hit my chest with a blow that threw me off balance. I was face down in the dust, the breath knocked from my body. Legs jostled around me and voices argued, and then I spotted the lackey's green breeches. I'd caught my breath now and I was furious. I grabbed one of the green legs and yanked hard. He tumbled down next to me.

I heard shrieks and looked up. The rider was raising his staff over Nicholas, and next to him, like some trusting dog, was the girl.

My heart was racing, I remember, and my body moved before

my mind could think. I picked up a stone and scrambled to my feet, arm half raised. That's when Nicholas glanced at me. He put his hand on my arm.

I don't know if the rider saw me or not. His eyes were moving over the mob of young people tightening around Nicholas like a cloak.

"We won't stay here long," Nicholas told him calmly.

The rider nodded. "Then I trust I'll have no need to summon the archbishop's men." His servant scowled at me and brushed the dust off his clothes, but said nothing. The man turned his horse away. I wonder now: was he glad to avoid a fight?

My anger drained away and I realized I was shaking. My mind seemed to have caught up with me at last and was asking what on earth I was doing.

Nicholas turned to me. "Will you join us?" he asked, simple as that.

It caught me off guard! Maybe my fall had dazed me—for a moment I couldn't answer. This was what I had come for, but I hesitated. I thought of my father. Was he already waiting for me? I could imagine him growing impatient, his face angry—or would it be anxious?

Nicholas was watching me. I pictured Otto and held on to the image of his face. And then I thought of Nicholas's words to the crowd and wondered, What if he's right? What if God wants him to gather a new kind of army? If I ignore this call and go home, what will happen to my soul? And if he succeeds—if I succeed—then a broken promise to my father or mother will surely be forgiven—won't it?

22nd day of June, 1212
On the March

My feet ache and my belly's empty, but I don't care. I'm sunburned and I've walked for an entire day, and I've never felt so good. If I had any doubts, they melted in the sun when we left Cologne far behind, following the Rhine. What a crowd we are already! Hundreds strong. I can still hear our steps crunching on the stony road.

In some ways we're an odd mixture, all following Nicholas: mostly boys, all ages, but some girls too.

TO THE CONCERNED BURGHERS AND GUILD MEMBERS, IN THE MATTER OF NICHOLAS OF COLOGNE

No wonder preachers can fire people up to join a cause. It's easy: peasants and villagers are always toiling, uncertain about the future, so it's simple to give a man, woman, or child an excuse to lose their head and go wild, like steam knocking off a lid. Much harder to control them, or guess what they'll do next!

I am an old man now and have written for our city's Royal Chronicle for many years. To monks and book-learned clerks like myself falls the task of noting all that happens nearby, and what we hear about from far away. (We used to do it in rhyme, but no one bothers with that anymore.) I know many strange stories that show how this case of the boy Nicholas, which so frightens you, is not the first one under the sun.

In the Year of Our Lord 1182, in the land of the French, a carpenter named Durand had a vision of Mary the mother of Our Lord Jesus, who gave him a scrap of parchment bearing a prayer for peace. Durand gathered a huge following and together they went after the robbers who plagued the local people. At first everyone, rich and poor, noble and serf, loved them. Once they turned on those who held power, however, things changed. Durand and his band were condemned and hunted down.

▶

There are older boys with the first signs of beards on their faces, even a couple of young mothers holding babies. Some boys carry banners (I'll save my strength for walking!), and others have pilgrim's staffs and leather pouches around their waists, hoping for donations. A few monks started walking alongside; I was happy to see their cart loaded with food. Everyone seems as excited as I am—by the pounding feet, the multitude we make, the road stretching ahead to who knows where.

There's one problem, though. The girl from Cologne, the one I pulled out of the rider's way—she's been following me like a shadow. Margarete is her name. We talked for a while, and I like her well enough, but I've started to keep my distance. I don't want to be unfriendly or mean, but I'm not here to be anyone's big brother. I didn't bring Gisela along, after all! I'm here for a reason, and it's best not to make it harder.

Whenever we pass peasants in the fields or villagers on the road, they look amazed, or sometimes afraid. They peek out of their cottages or drop their scythes and stare. "Bless you!" some of them call, or they cross themselves. Sometimes they grip their own children, as if they'd like to hide them from us. But a few women have run up to push bundles of food into our hands. One farmer shouted, "Where are you going?"

"To God!" Nicholas answered, and everybody echoed him.

Following Nicholas   2 of 2

Before that, in the year 1096, during the first campaign to Jerusalem, a ragged holy man known as Peter the Hermit got all the lowly people excited. A motley band of peasants without weapons—even old men, and women with babies—followed him to the Holy Land. They had no commander of any worth to lead them and ignored all those who tried to discourage them. As soon as they got anywhere near the Turkish armies, they were ambushed and scattered like leaves.

Oh, there are many stories of this kind. In 1075, 16 men and women started dancing outside the church in Kölbigk when they should have been at morning prayers. After the priest scolded them, they kept dancing for a year! Their dancing feet dug a trench in the ground, and still they danced, until the pit was up to their hips. The Bishop of Cologne is said to have released them from the fit. That one might be a legend, though.

The strangest thing of all took place in the town of Hameln. It makes me shiver to tell it. On the day of Saint John and Saint Paul, a handsome man in fine clothes came over the bridge and through the city gates. He played a silver flute, and every boy who heard it followed him out of the gate—130 boys in all, they say. Though all the parents searched and searched, no one could ever find them.

Three Paths in the World

The Priest, the Knight, and the Laborer stand for the three kinds of life a person may lead in this world. The priest prays, the knight fights, and the laborer works with his hands to plant, craft, or build. Each has a role to play both at home and in the struggles for the Holy Land. While it is the knight who is called to go forth and fight there, the other two sustain and help him: the priest with his prayers, the laborer with the food and goods he provides.

After that happened, Nicholas turned around and caught my eye. He tilted his head, as if to show I should join him. I could feel the eyes of the others on me, especially Margarete's, as I trotted up ahead. I tried not to let it show how good it felt to be singled out. Cause no one's envy, fear no one's wrath, my father says.

"See?" Nicholas said, waving his hand toward the fields. "They all believe in us."

I agreed, and then I blurted out how tired I was of grown men—my father and the other villagers—always telling the young that they're not ready, not needed yet.

Nicholas looked at me for a moment and then said, "Yes, they do say that. But don't forget, we're told 'the meek will inherit the Earth.' Aren't they God's chosen ones? And aren't the young and the poor meek?"

What else did we talk about? I don't ever want to forget a word of it. He asked me about my family and I told him about my father and how he wouldn't understand this; how he says it's enough for each man to know his trade and to do it well (words I could repeat in my sleep, I've heard them so often).

Nicholas said he'd been taught that a person can choose one of three paths in the world: to pray (like the monks), to work (like my father or the peasants we pass all day), or to fight (like the knights, like Otto). Of course, I've heard that too. But then he surprised me. He said there is really only one path: to serve. And God will reveal your purpose to you.

A couple of other things from today stand out in my mind. When we stopped at the riverside to fill our flasks, I heard horses' hooves. A group of boys and young men were heading down the riverbank toward us, three on horseback. Their clothes were fine, and I thought how odd they looked next to all the barefoot children. They came right up to Nicholas. I straightened up. I confess, I wanted them to know I was with *him*.

One of them offered Nicholas his horse, but he shook his head. Good for him, I thought. We're all walking—why shouldn't he? The boy insisted. Then one of his friends started in, loud and important-sounding, as if he were giving us all a speech. He was stocky and had neatly cut hair the color of pale wheat. "You'll inspire the crowd if they can all see you," he said.

Nicholas frowned and hesitated, then he nodded. A small part of me was disappointed, but I'm sure Nicholas knows best. A few people grumbled, and I gave them a hard look. Who are they to judge him? I didn't talk to Nicholas again after that, since of course he started riding at the head of the group.

As for the loudmouth who convinced Nicholas to mount, I got a taste of his forward ways soon enough. We passed some trades-men on the road who cheered us, and one of them pressed a few coins into my hand. "God bless you," he said. I was so startled by the silver in my palm that I barely remembered to thank him.

Gunter (that's the loud one's name) was at my elbow in a flash. "We can't have everyone carrying the donations," he said. He opened the pouch on his belt. "I've already started collecting, so hand it over."

I felt my face get hot.

"My father's a merchant," he added, "so I'm used to handling money."

What did his father have to do with it? What's my father, then—a fool? I didn't mean to start fighting with him. I really didn't care who carried the coins. But I didn't like someone pushing his face into mine, telling me what to do. It started with words, but I guess my temper got the best of me, and an instant later we were shoving each other. Suddenly Nicholas was between us, pushing us apart, and I felt ashamed.

At dusk a handful of men fell into step with us. Gunter gave them a sideways look, and said something about keeping an eye on them. That was too much! He'd just turned up himself, and now he was going to pick and choose who joined?

"It won't hurt to have their help," I said, loud enough for him to hear.

23rd day of June, 1212
Harsh Lesson

Last night a farmer let some of us sleep in his barn. At first light I heard voices shouting outside. One of the boys stood there staring at the leather pouch in his hand, blinking away tears, as if he couldn't believe it. All the money he'd collected was gone. And so are the men who joined us yesterday.

30th day of June, 1212
Into the Woods

I had a taste of real fear today, not just of getting lost, but of being left behind. The whole time I kept thinking, How will I ever find Otto without them, without Nicholas?

We'd left a village far behind us, and by midday it was so hot that at first I was glad when I saw the forest ahead: shade at last! Soon the thick trunks towered all around us. The path was so deep in trees that I lost sight of Nicholas. People darted ahead and seemed to disappear on the other side of the firs. A few of us were walking in a tight group, with Gunter giving orders.

"Come on, come on," he kept saying through clenched teeth. "We've got to catch up."

I was following too (I may not like Gunter taking charge, but I'm not fool enough to fall behind), when someone called my name. Margarete again. She was trotting after us. I waited for her, my legs itching to get moving, keeping one eye on the others, who were already halfway up a slope and almost out of sight. I grabbed her hand as soon as she was within reach and pulled her up the hill.

But we were too late. It was as if everyone had been swallowed up by the trees. I looked at the ground. Our path had already dwindled to a trail, but now, at the top of the slope, it was gone altogether. I had no idea which was the right way. Neither did Margarete.

Margarete! This was her fault. I was angry with her, but one look at her frightened face convinced me not to show it.

"Come this way," I said, pretending to know where I was going. Better any choice than none, I thought.

I don't know how long we walked. I couldn't even track time by the sun; the trees kept us in twilight. I'm a bit ashamed now to admit it, but my mind was swimming with stories my mother had told me and Gisela when we were very young, about the creatures that live deep in the woods. I could almost see them: the horrible faces of the trolls who used to grin at me in nightmares.

Stop it! I kept telling myself. Didn't Otto say those were just stupid tales made up to frighten children into staying close to home? Margarete's arm kept bumping against mine and I knew she was scared too. She pointed to a tree and asked in a low voice if we had seen it before. I shook my head, but my heart sank. Were we walking in circles? How long until nightfall?

I was wondering what Otto would do, when something bright caught my eye: a patch of light gray past the black trunks. The color of poplar bark. I thought of how I'd walked with Father along the sunny riverside to find poplar wood for carving or burning. It wasn't sturdy enough for a wheel; the stronger wood grew deep in the forest.

Then I remembered. Poplars need sun and water. They grow at the forest's edge, usually near a river. I nearly laughed out loud. I pushed through the fir boughs toward the bright trees, Margarete at my heels.

I was right! The trees began to thin and I could feel the late-day sun again. Margarete let out a shout of happiness. Ahead the river shimmered, and voices—the others—were singing in the distance.

Relief washed over me like rain, but I felt something else too—triumph. I glanced at Margarete, and I admit I expected her to look grateful or even admiring. But she wasn't looking at me at all. She was staring ahead with a serious expression.

"Look," she said, her eyes bright. She held out something in her palm. It was a small image of a saint, carved in amber.

"It was my mother's," she explained. "While we walked, I was praying to Saint Christopher, the guide of all travelers. He answered our prayer with a miracle."

I opened my mouth to explain about the trees, but when I saw how happy she looked, I changed my mind. Maybe in a way she's right. Maybe that *is* what they call a miracle.

5th day of July, 1212
Sea of Faces

I'm too tired to think much tonight. I see less and less of Nicholas all the time. The crowd of followers has swelled. There are thousands of us. We sprawl across the land, clustered in groups. Shepherds' and peasants' children leave their flocks and fields to join us when we pass. I met a new boy yesterday who said his mother had tried to stop him. She bolted the door, but he got out through the window. Some speak a language I don't understand; I think they are French. It took me by surprise when, among all the strangers, I saw a familiar face from home—an older boy who left Wiesdorf years ago to be a miller's apprentice. He thought I was Otto at first!

All these people, they come and go, and it's hard to keep track of everyone. I've already lost sight of the miller boy. And the heat is hard to bear. This is the driest, hottest summer I can remember. Most of the boys are tougher than they look, and there's not too much complaining. I expected Margarete would drop behind, but she's stronger than she looks too. If she's tired, she never says.

Gunter is another story. He doesn't exactly complain, but he always plants the seed that gets others grumbling. Yesterday he hinted that Nicholas never seems to be here when we need him most, and that set some of the younger ones sniveling.

"Nicholas can't be everywhere at once," I shot back. "And besides, he can count on us."

At least, on some of us, I could have added.

20th day of July, 1212
A Different Army

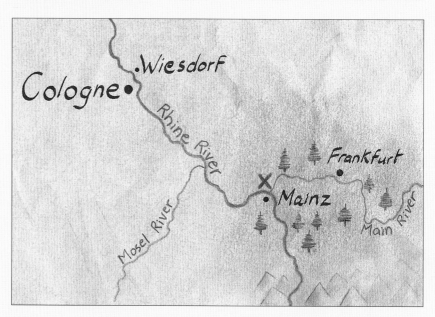

I saw him again! I mean the stranger, the one who came to our house in the night. I wish I hadn't. But that's only part of it. Let me start at the beginning.

We reached Mainz and I was glad to be back in a city, especially once Margarete told me that her mother's cousins lived there. I was looking forward to sleeping in a house!

I asked her if she was worried they would tell her to go home, and she told me her mother had left this world. As for her father,

To the Noble Lords of the French Lands of Normandy, Anjou, Blois, and Burgundy

To take the cross now means more than fighting in the Holy Land. It has come to mean facing any threat against the Church, as long as Pope Innocent has so named it.

As you surely know, the Albigensians, or Cathars, are called heretics by our Church. They say they strive for spiritual purity, and take it so far that they call all flesh evil and deny that Jesus was ▶

Simon of Montfort

he stayed in the fields and with the flocks as much as he could, and was always angry when he was home. She guessed he was glad she was gone; there were too many of them to feed. She said it without sounding bitter at all, as if she had accepted it long ago. I felt ashamed then that I haven't been kinder to her.

I pictured my own mother and father, and for a moment my throat tightened in a painful way. I knew they weren't glad I was gone, and I wondered if they were searching for me. Or had they given up by now? I quickly pushed those thoughts away. What I needed to do was find Otto, then all would be well again.

Margarete's cousins were friendly to her, but the father of the household eyed me coldly. I felt nervous in their house and out of place. So when his wife asked someone to fetch water, I offered to go.

I followed the path she pointed out to the well, away from the houses and down a hill. Some of Nicholas's older followers were leaning on the stone well, looking dusty and tired. I'd nodded to them and was lowering my bucket when I noticed a pack of men leading their horses toward us. They were dusty from the road too, but they were no pilgrims. They were all armed for war, except for one who wore a monk's robes. He called out to the boys and asked how old they were.

"Sixteen years," one answered. (I think he was lying.) I recognized him; he was the one who had given up his horse to Nicholas. Peter—that's his name.

"Old enough," the monk said, "to take up the cross alongside men on a blessed mission. One," he added loudly, "sanctioned by the Church."

Another one of the travelers, a man with a blond beard and a long scar on his face, said they were riding to Puylaurens to join Simon of Montfort. He had raised a mighty army to crush the heretics in the south of France.

With a jolt I remembered the stranger's talk in our house. I stared at the men, and then I saw *him*, still on his horse, behind the others. It had been dark the first time I saw him, but I was sure it was the same broad face, the same eyes. The next instant his gaze locked on mine and he frowned, as if trying to remember if he knew me.

Siege

heretics for forty days was promised the same forgiveness of sins as one who'd gone to the Holy Land. We set out with a strong army—a duke, three counts, and three archbishops were among our leaders. One Albigensian lord was so frightened he rushed to confess, take the cross, and join us as we moved along the Rhône River.

At the first city we besieged, some defenders snuck out, and we grabbed the chance to force the gate. We were merciless to everyone within, heretic or not, so as to spread fear through the surrounding lands. It worked: town after town surrendered as we marched toward the last stubborn holdout, the walled city of Carcassonne. That <u>siege</u> ended in surrender too, and we let those inside leave bearing nothing but their sins.

Their forty days up, the nobles left for home, and I remained in command of a small army—not, as some say, to make myself more powerful by taking over the lands I conquered. The heretics are not yet stamped out, and rebellion grows. My brave but small force cannot overcome them alone. I await your arrival, along with all the men you can compel or pay to join our cause.

Simon of Montfort,
En route to the rebel city of Toulouse

ever a flesh-and-blood man. In the south of France, many nobles have joined them, either secretly or openly.

Pope Innocent first tried to stamp out these ideas by sending the preacher Dominic and his friars. At last he gave up and called upon the French nobles. Any man who would fight the

I turned to Peter. "Tell him," I said. "Tell him *our* cause is the true one."

But he didn't. He asked the riders questions, and the other boys started too. They were curious and excited and didn't hide it. I grabbed one of them by the arm, but he shook me off. The blond rider laughed at that. The boys crowded around the riders and stuck to them as they began to leave. I called after them, but they ignored me. Where was Nicholas? I couldn't stop them, but he could.

I turned to run and find him, but a hand clapped on my shoulder. It was the stranger. I never even saw him dismount. He must have guessed that I was going to raise some kind of alarm or find someone who would hinder them. For the first time I noticed how lonely the spot was.

This next part still makes my face burn. But I started out to tell the truth about everything that happens, so I won't stop now. I squirmed and fought to get out of the stranger's grasp, but his grip was like an iron vise. He clamped his other hand over my mouth. The blond rider was suddenly at his side, and the two of them tied my hands and feet and stuffed a rag in my mouth.

"This fish is still too small—let's throw him back in the stream," the stranger said, and his friend laughed. They dropped me to the ground and left. I could see Peter and the others leaving with the men; none of them looked back.

I'm not sure how long I stayed there, boiling with anger and shame. I made as much noise as I could, but no one heard my muffled shouting, or no one came if they did. (Did the townspeople here fear us, or just wish us gone?)

It was Margarete who found me at last. I heard her calling my name, and to me it was a beautiful sound! Her eyes widened like an owl's when she saw me, but she set to work untying me. She was quick and nimble at it.

She must have asked me questions, but I hardly heard her. My only thought was that I had to find Nicholas in time. I pushed past her and raced up the path, past the houses, I don't know where. I turned a corner and smacked up against—not Nicholas—but Gunter.

Well, here's someone forceful enough to haul them all back, I thought. I tried to tell him quickly what had happened, but I didn't want to waste any more time, and I may have babbled.

"We have to make them stay together. We can't let it all break up," I ranted, tugging on his arm, but he was like a post stuck in the ground. "Nicholas is counting on us!"

What did I expect? I don't know, but I thought he would be angry enough to storm after them. Instead, he shrugged.

"We're all going the same way for now," he said. He even seemed glad to be rid of them. Or was I imagining that? "More glory for us," I think he said.

But then he asked me questions about the armed men. He seemed keen to know more. What was he up to? Something flashed across my mind that made the hair on my neck stand up. Was Gunter here to follow Nicholas, or did he have another plan?

When I got back to the house, Margarete was there, her face anxious. Her questions bothered me, and we argued. I asked her why she couldn't just stay with her cousins. This venture was getting dangerous, and I was out of patience. How could I survive with her trailing behind me? At that, she stopped looking worried about me; she looked furious. "I can take care of myself," she snapped.

I'm not so sure. How can she stay safe, when I can't?

A Monk's Life

Greetings to you, dear brother and sister in Christ!

Many thanks for your message asking that your youngest son enter our monastery at Marbach. I have a few words of advice for your boy.

Rules laid down by Saint Benedict

Like most monks, we follow the rules laid down by Saint Benedict in the 500s. He wrote what he called a "little rule for beginners," and promised it demanded "nothing harsh." He taught how a monk should spend his days:

Since you've given up everything you own, you are now free of all worldly concerns and can divide your day between prayer, work, and study. Don't pray only ▶

25th day of July, 1212
Monks and Worldly Kings

A good meal at last! And all for an easy bit of work on a monk's wheel. A small band of us—20 or so—passed him on the road, with his donkey and broken cart. Margarete offered my help to him, since she knows I'm a wheelwright's son. I couldn't help scowling at her. I'm hardly a master; Father's taught me such little, stupid things so far. Unless the Brother needs someone to sweep the sawdust off his floor, I thought, I won't be much use.

Sometimes a little luck is all you need. It turned out to be such a simple matter to fix—an axle had wobbled out of the hub—that I almost laughed. But I kept a serious face when he thanked me so gratefully. Maybe I've learned more than I thought.

My deed earned our group a free supper at the monastery, so for a while I was everyone's hero—even Gunter's. I wondered if we'd all have to bow our heads and eat in silence, but our meal at the long table was noisy with laughing and talking.

Good bread and fish in my stomach raised my spirits, and I'm afraid it loosened my tongue as well. I've been feeling bad about how I treated Margarete in Mainz after she helped me. So at supper I told her about Otto. Until now I've kept all my plans about finding him to myself, and it's a lonely feeling to have something

when you feel like it: stop and pray with others seven times a day, then get up in the middle of the night and pray again. In between prayers, work hard in the orchard and fields (idleness breeds evil), but also study. (One of your important jobs is to write or copy precious books.)

Live in a community with other monks (not a hermit's hut), because putting up with others' faults brings you closer to God and reminds you that you are not perfect either. Remember, not too much talking while you work, and no rude jokes! Talking just to make someone else laugh is to be avoided. So is too much of any-thing, including food and drink. At the two meals you eat together each day, two dishes are enough. (If you don't like one, you can eat the other.)

Welcome all travelers and pilgrims: your monastery is a safe haven in a dangerous world. But if someone arrives wanting to be a monk, be rude to him and refuse to let him in for five days, just to be sure he's serious.

Remember, the worst kinds of monks are those who live alone or in small groups with no rules or Abbot (a superior in charge of everyone), and who think that whatever they feel like doing is God's will. Even worse: those who travel from monastery to monastery enjoying big free meals. Gluttons! Only those who have grown strong living under rules are able to live as hermits with only God helping them.

Brother Markus

Saint Benedict and his followers.

WHO HOLDS THE POWER IN 1212: A GUIDE FOR VISITORS TO THE ROYAL COURTS OF CHRISTENDOM

Otto IV, Holy Roman Emperor

The emperor's title is meant to show that he is the successor of the Roman emperors and God's deputy for leading everyone in worldly matters, whereas the Pope is in charge of the spiritual. The Holy Roman Empire includes many lands in the middle of Europe, and is intended to unite Christian peoples under one rule.

The Pope crowned Otto emperor in 1209 (he was one of two rival German kings), but excommunicated, or banned, him from the Church the next year for trying to conquer Sicily. The French king and German princes are trying to topple Otto from power, and it's not likely he'll be emperor much longer.

Pope Innocent III

In 1198 this young Italian became Pope—the Bishop of Rome and spiritual leader of the Western Christian church. Energetic and good at persuading rulers, he is active in politics as well as religion and influences every country in Europe. His support can determine which of two rival nobles will be crowned king. He is making the role of Pope more powerful than ever. ▶

always on your mind without being able to tell anyone. As soon as the words were out of my mouth, though, I regretted it. Nicholas thinks I'm here for his reasons, and I am, in a way—only he might not see it like that. And I don't trust Gunter. Something told me that I should have kept Otto to myself. I asked Margarete not to tell anyone, and she nodded so solemnly that I don't think she will. But there was a gleam in her eye, too, as if she was thrilled to have a secret to keep.

Our talk was cut short. The Abbot strode in and stood at the head of the table. He commended us all for our bravery and spirit. And then he told us to go home!

He called our venture "reckless." Without the guidance of our "betters," he said, it is doomed. His next words nearly knocked me off my bench: our emperor himself and the French king both oppose us.

All down the table there was confusion, everyone talking at once, everyone asking questions. I couldn't believe it. Kings were noticing us, were even worried about our plan! I grabbed the sleeve of the monk whose wheel I'd mended and asked him if it was true. He nodded. Stories of our mission have spread. The French king is against us because he believes the Evil One, not God, inspired Nicholas. The German emperor, my monk told me in a lower voice, was no friend to any venture that would make the Pope more powerful.

Well, the reasons of <u>rulers</u>, their friendships and hatreds—these are things beyond me, I know that. All I can do is judge what is in front of me as right or wrong. And what we're doing, what Nicholas is doing, is plainly right. It's so simple—how could anyone twist it into something evil?

I looked around at the shocked faces. Someone had to speak up for our side. I could already see what would happen: just as in Mainz, there'd be deserters again. We'd lose half our ranks before we even reached the sea. And again, no Nicholas! I'd seen no sign of him for days.

One glance at Gunter across the table made up my mind. I stood up and cleared my throat loudly. Everyone stared, even the Abbot.

"It is not for earthly kings that we have taken up this cross,"

King Philip II of France

Crowned in 1180, he led an army to the Holy Land along with Richard the Lionheart of England and the old Holy Roman Emperor, but had to return home when he became sick.

Otto IV, Holy Roman Emperor

Pope Innocent III

King Philip II of France

King of Jerusalem, Jean de Brienne

King of Jerusalem, Jean de Brienne

This French count became king of Christian territory in the Holy Land in 1212 by marrying Mary, the heir to the Kingdom of Jerusalem (with the support of King Philip and the Pope).

After the Christian forces lost Jerusalem in 1187, the center of their kingdom moved to Acre. Some of the rulers since then have been kings in name only. Unless Jean has a strong personality, he will not easily control the powerful knightly orders in the Holy Land.

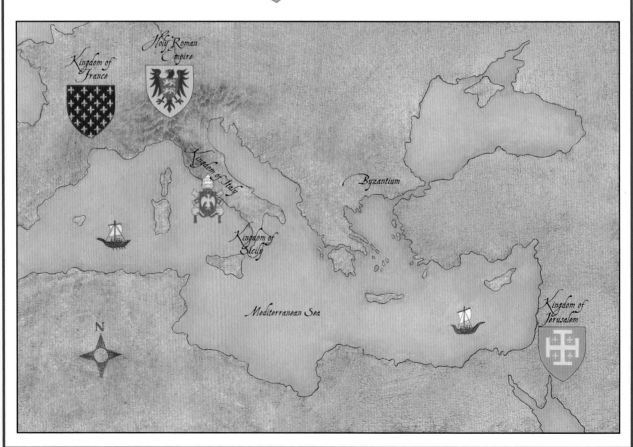

I said (praying my voice wouldn't shake). "We thank you for this food and welcome, but our course is decided."

Where did I get those words from? I have no idea. I sat down heavily before anyone could see my hands trembling. There was a pause, then heads were nodding (Gunter's too, I saw). One of the boys started pounding his palm on the table in agreement, and others did the same.

We didn't stay the night. When we walked out through the monks' orchards, I felt a little regret: no roof to sleep under. We headed toward grassy hills, and beyond those I saw mountaintops, blue in the distance. Of course, I've heard of the famous mountains that lie across our path to Italy and the sea, but I'd never seen them, and until now they didn't seem real. How are we ever going to cross them?

Sometimes I wish I could just have faith, like Margarete. Or Otto—I can't count how often he told me stories of this or that saint or miracle, with a faraway look in his eyes I could never understand. As for me, one moment I feel I could fly if Nicholas said I could (the way I felt talking to the Abbot) and the next I feel, well, what I feel when I look at those towering mountains.

27th day of July, 1212
God's Plan

Just a few words before I sleep. From a hilltop today I spotted a motley group on the road ahead, and among them that familiar head of tangled dark hair. Nicholas, at last! I nearly sprinted down the hill. He clapped me on the shoulder and we talked the way we did that first day, on the road outside Cologne. Now I know we can do anything.

The only troubling part: I tried to warn him about Gunter and what happened in Mainz. Maybe I was clumsy in telling it. He cut me off in the middle of my story, shaking his head as if he wanted to keep my words out of his ears. He told me not to judge Gunter. "I've only set things in motion," he said. "God has his own plan for us, and has chosen all his agents for a reason."

It bothers me, I can't help it, and that's why I'm still awake while everyone is snoring around me. For one thing, I thought

Nicholas trusted me, and that, well, I know it sounds foolish, but that maybe I could be his helper, his right hand. But more than that, I'm not convinced inside that he's right about this one thing, even though I know he must be. I just don't *feel* that he is.

2nd day of August, 1212
Climbing Skyward

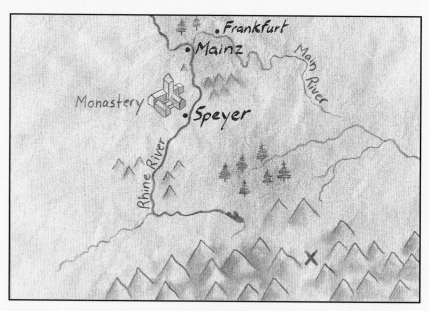

When I try to breathe deeply, I gasp and my head spins. Gunter (who knows everything, it seems) tells me it's the mountain air. This made no sense to me—air is air. But I have no better explanation for why I am always out of breath.

For days now we walk upward, always upward. There are no more trails. My thin leather shoes and breeches are in tatters. It gets colder as we climb, and I shiver now in the same wool smock that made me sweat on the roads along the Rhine. For hours today our path ran alongside a gorge. I glanced down once and felt so dizzy I reached out to steady myself against the mountain face. The stones cut my hand.

At one point I thought that, from above, we must look like a long snake inching its way forward, painfully slow. The idea made me giddy and I must have laughed out loud, because a couple of boys glanced back at me, and even Margarete looked at me oddly.

I bit my lip. Anyway, who would be looking at us from above? God, I remind myself.

At night, around our fire of turf and twigs, they start—the doubters, the complainers. Maybe our mothers were right, they mutter. What if Nicholas is wrong? What if he's not following God at all? What if he brought us here just to perish in the cold? And on and on. Don't they know it's better to leave some things unsaid? When I think of who starts it each time, I always picture Gunter. Or am I imagining that? It's not so bad when Nicholas is with us. He finds the words to calm fears or fire up faith. And most of them don't dare grumble in front of him. When he's not here, I try to do the talking, but it's not the same. My words don't sound convincing, even to me.

To make matters worse—and I'm almost afraid to put this into words—Margarete has changed. She's weaker. Sometimes the way gets so steep I have to drag her after me, and I can hear the rasping sound her breathing makes now. But, like always, she never complains. I tell myself that if faith can save, then she will be all right, because hers is much stronger than mine.

6th day of August, 1212
A New Ally?

Help comes from unexpected places. Or maybe that's another kind of miracle, the kind Margarete sees everywhere.

We were moving slowly up a steep rock face, and I was half helping, half pushing Margarete. I'd grab hold of her slipping leg, or hold her by the back while she caught her breath. It was tiring! Sweat was stinging my eyes and running in rivers down my back. My hands were slick and Margarete started to feel even heavier. She was tiring out too; she'd stopped trying.

Suddenly, I couldn't go any farther. There was nothing left to grab hold of, nothing to pull up on, nothing to push off from. I could see the legs of those above us disappear overhead, but I was stuck. Margarete froze, as if she knew without a word that we were in trouble. No way up, no way down, and I could feel her weight sinking against me more and more.

We're going to fall, I thought. And then—it felt like magic at the time—her weight lifted, as if she had grown wings. I blinked away the sweat in my eyes and looked up to see arms reaching down, pulling her. It was Gunter.

My relief lasted about the time it takes to breathe in and out. Margarete kicked wildly as she rose, and rocks tumbled down. Little ones at first, then bigger. Before I knew it, my hands were holding nothing at all and I was sliding down on my belly. My foot hit something hard and I stopped.

I was out of reach of Gunter or anyone, teetering like a loose weather vane, balancing on my stomach. Gunter shouted something, lost in the wind. He shouted it again, and this time I heard: "Kick off your shoes."

I understood. I needed an extra pair of hands to grip with. Leather soles can't grip. I kicked hard and shook them off and clawed my way up, panting, testing each foothold before I hoisted myself up a little more. Gunter was stretched over the rocky ledge above, watching and waiting. When I was within reach, he held down his hand. I took it and I trusted him. I suddenly knew I could, even if it was just this once. Or maybe I had no other choice.

We rested for a while, saying nothing, then we looked at each other and barely nodded. We had to get moving again. The way ahead was still steep, but it could be walked. Only now, some of the younger ones refused to get up. Gunter, being Gunter, nudged them none too gently with his foot.

"No," they said, "no more." They started praying, and others joined them. What were they going to do? Stay here in the wind and cold and pray to be rescued?

"You have to save yourselves," Gunter shouted. "We all do."

I agreed. Staying here was madness. We pushed and goaded them upward.

I hate to admit this, even to myself, but Gunter has a certain kind of strength, and now I've seen that he can put it to good use, at least sometimes. He even found me shoes for my bleeding feet. I asked him who their owner was.

He looked at me and said, "One who no longer needs them."

I didn't ask any more; I don't dare think too much. But I wore them.

Yes, he could be someone you'd want by your side. As long as he is *on* your side.

10th day of August, 1212
Torn Asunder

My head is spinning—there's so much to tell. We're through the mountains, thank God. We're fewer now, and ragged, like beggars,

Franks in Constantinople

I, Niketas Choniates, a Greek, saw firsthand <u>the plunder of the city of Constantinople</u> by the Frankish army. I swear that all that follows is true.

The Venetians and Franks broke through the walls on the fourth day of the siege. I am lucky to have escaped with my life. (I know that an army on the move takes what it needs from the cities it conquers. And I know that a city that holds out during a siege can expect less mercy than one that surrenders quickly. But what I witnessed has no possible defense.)

News spread rapidly that our new emperor had abandoned his throne, which caused panic. The city was ransacked for three days. The soldiers took whatever they wanted and attacked anyone who stood in their way. They did not stop at people's belongings, but broke into the great church of St. Sofia.

They carried off the sacred objects, all the fine works in silver and gold, every ornament they could. They stripped the altar and the mighty doors bare of their gold and precious materials. There was too much to carry out themselves, so they led their horses right into the sanctuary, where the beasts slipped on the tiles.

▶

but that didn't matter when we finally looked down into the greenest valley I've ever seen. The Kingdom of Italy—and the sea! Nicholas smiled at me, and I felt the way I did when I found him in the foothills past the monastery: like we could do anything.

The first thing we needed to take care of was food. If I've learned anything from Gunter, it's to be practical. We drew lots, and while everyone else rested, two boys headed for a town we'd spotted from the foothills to scout for bread, drink—anything.

Our peaceful Eden on the grassy slope didn't last long. My eyes were closed and I was lying back on the grass when it started: voices arguing, like a fly buzzing when you're trying to sleep. Then Gunter shouting at Nicholas. My eyes flew open.

"That's how the last great army found a way to the Holy Land," Gunter was saying. "East to Venice and the sea. And that's where we should go too!" His voice was harsh and he talked to Nicholas as if he were his equal. No, as if he were an opponent, someone he had to defeat.

Nicholas was shaking his head. "The Venice merchants will demand a fortune for our passage," he said. "The knights you speak of sold their loyalties to get a ship, and how did that end? With <u>the sacking of a Christian city</u>.

"We'll follow this road west to the sea," he added firmly.

"We can all decide for ourselves!" Gunter barked. He turned to face the others. "I'm for Venice. Who's with me?"

No one had time to answer. Our two scouts were heading back to us, running hard, as if the Devil himself were on their heels.

They were panting and both talked at once. They'd been chased from the town. While we were in the mountains, cut off from all human souls, a war had begun. Italian forces were now battling German ones, goodness knows where, and the townspeople had heard frightening stories of a "horde" of northerners marching south. It took me a moment to realize they meant us—then I nearly laughed, scared as I was. If they could only see us, tattered and unarmed! But it was no joke. The men in town were gathering weapons as we spoke, preparing to drive us back.

I wonder if things might have turned out differently if there had been time for Nicholas to speak, to calm everyone. We might have stayed together. But there was no time for anything but escape.

The Sacking of a Christian City   2 of 2

An abbot among the invading army was seen helping himself to sacred relics, and hurried back to his ship with a piece of the Cross and relics of over a dozen martyrs. When the soldiers shouted to him from the ships, asking how he had fared, he answered, "We've done well today!"

The Venetians bore away many, many treasures to adorn their own city.

The plunder of the city of Constantinople

There'd be no pity for us, no chance to explain, even if they spoke our language.

As if a blade had dropped through our core, the group split in two. People made their choice in the time it takes to blink: Nicholas or Gunter; run west or east.

Gunter caught my eye. "Come with us," he called.

I shook my head. He glanced briefly at Margarete, who had leaned against me, coughing. Then he quickly turned away and was gone. Margarete and I headed after Nicholas. His panicking followers were already passing us. I still couldn't believe he wasn't stopping this disaster.

Margarete stumbled and I barely caught her as she slumped down. I said her name, but she didn't answer. I put my head next to hers. Her breaths were coming in short gasps. I knew I had to get her somewhere safe. I remembered the stone buildings I'd seen from the hills, west of the town. A holy order? Well, I would have to hope so. We couldn't stay here.

Nicholas was already out of sight. He'll have no idea where I've gone, I thought. He'll think I left with Gunter. But I'd have to worry about that later.

I half carried Margarete, staggering by the time I reached the low stone wall. I found a wooden door with a cross on it and pounded.

After what seemed like an age, it opened and a nun in her long dark garment looked out. When I spoke, she shook her head; she didn't understand me. I started explaining with my hands, but she just stared at Margarete and, with a frown of alarm, motioned for us to follow her inside.

We carried Margarete to a cot. The nun began to speak to me in strange, flowing words I didn't understand. She pointed to the ground, twice. Yes, I nodded, of course, she should stay here.

There, I thought, I've done all I can. My legs were itching to be off after Nicholas. But now Margarete's drowsy eyes sprang open. "No, no," she said.

Did she want to come with me? Or for me to stay? I still don't know, but both were impossible. "You'll be safe here," I said. I felt guilty. But what else could I do?

She reached out her hand and I took it. She was pressing something into my palm, and I saw it was her saint's medal, the one she believed had saved us in the forest. I promised to come back for her. Now I don't know if that was wise, or right. Can I promise anything when I know so little about my own future?

22nd day of August, 1212
City of Gold

So this is the sea. At last I've seen it. I'm in a strange city and I feel farther from home than ever. Genoa, it's called. The light on the water, on the brightly painted houses, dazzles me and I feel almost giddy. But I've caught up with Nicholas at last.

I saw his followers from a distance, thousands milling about outside Genoa's walls. I learned from them that the city council refused to open the gates to us. They were scared of our numbers, afraid we'd gobble up everything and steal what we weren't given. But they had let Nicholas inside and he was pleading with them. When at last he reappeared, he said they were letting us in—for one night! There were groans all around, but Nicholas shouted that it was all we needed; God would find a way for us across the water in the morning.

How? I wondered, but I kept that to myself. I was glad to hear Nicholas sounding so confident, just as bold as he had been in Cologne.

Once inside the city, everyone fanned out through the streets. We ate and drank as much as we wanted for our single day; it was like a carnival. I ate happily with the rest and looked around.

I remembered the stone cathedral in Cologne, and it seemed dark and plain compared to this golden city. A group of the youngest boys crowded around a juggler. One of them ran to me and tugged at my sleeve.

"Is this Jerusalem?" he asked.

I laughed, but then a voice in my head scolded me. We had come for a reason, not to cram sweets in our mouths. I set out to

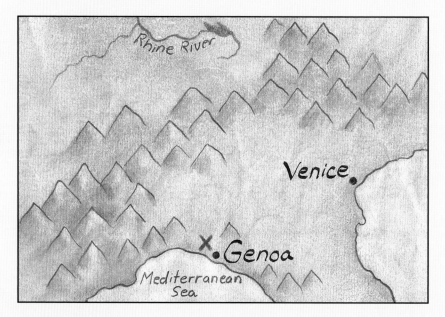

find Nicholas. He was stalking the waterside like a dog trailing a scent. I joined him, and we searched for someone who would give us passage.

No one would. Well, one merchant unloading his ship listened to us for a heartbeat, but as soon as we admitted we had no money, he waved us away. The sailors looked at us like we were rats trying to board their ship.

I saw a rider moving along the quay, hunched over his horse. When he got closer, I spotted a ragged cross sewn on the front of his shirt. He reined in his horse and dismounted slowly, as if the effort hurt him. Whoever he was, he'd taken the cross. Could he help us?

I pointed him out to Nicholas and we approached him. Nicholas asked him where he was going.

"Home," he said simply. He was German!

I asked if he had been to Jerusalem. He told us he had been as far as Sidon and Beirut, and fought there. The names meant nothing to me, but my heart was pounding. He had really been *there*! To the Holy Land. Imagine the stories a man like this could tell—and he would know things, about others there, about Otto.

I started spitting out questions, I hardly know what. I asked him if the Muslim armies were as terrible as people said. He said they were men, no better or worse than others. What kind of answer was that? A riddle?

His face hardened into a frown and he told us to leave him alone. Now I was afraid he'd leave before I could learn anything about Otto. I quickly described the expedition of young men who had left the north for the Holy Land two years ago. He started to lead his horse away, but I followed as I talked. He snorted, a sound that was part laughter, part sigh.

"Newcomers are often more trouble than they're worth," he said. "The men you describe sound like a thousand others."

Talking quickly, I blurted out everything I could remember about Otto—that he was like me, only taller and older. The rider never glanced back, but I didn't stop. I told him about the light iron sword our blacksmith had made for Otto. I remembered that Ulrich had marked the blade with the sign of a wheel, and I told him about that too.

The man paused and half turned. I saw a glint flash across his eyes. "Fine work, that one," he muttered, almost too low to hear. "Roughly made, but strong."

My heart raced. I wondered if I'd misheard. I clutched his sleeve. "So you remember?"

He pulled away and shook his head. "I remember more than I care to," he said, scowling again. "And nothing to help you. Go home, boy." He winced as he mounted his horse and rode away from us.

I didn't notice at the time that Nicholas had grown very quiet. Later he seemed angry with me. He asked me what I hoped to learn from a man who had failed. He sounded sullen, as if I were siding against him. I was about to explain, when a guilty feeling crept over me. I've never told Nicholas my first reason for joining him. Now I wonder if that was lying. He trusts me. Did I mislead him?

By day's end, I was exhausted. Here we were—we'd reached the sea, but with no way to cross it. I didn't believe it was over, but neither could I see any way forward.

"Trust God, not me," Nicholas said, as if he could read the doubts on my face. "Didn't God part the waters of the Red Sea so the Hebrews could escape the Pharaoh's army and flee Egypt?"

"Yes," I said, "but what does that mean for us?" Was he saying that God would part the Mediterranean and we would walk to Jerusalem? I know that's exactly what many of the boys believe, especially the young ones.

Nicholas didn't answer me directly. "God will find a way," he said. He kept staring at my face, as if still reading doubts there, and I turned red. He told me to keep faith. Dawn will bring our answer.

23rd day of August, 1212
Crossroads

When I woke up this morning, half the boys who'd camped in the granary along with me were gone. Outside, the waterfront was quiet. It was eerie.

The sun was rising, brightening waters that had not parted. I never truly believed they would, but I had expected, well, something. What? I even caught myself looking up at the sky to see if a storm was on the way to begin our miracle. But it was blue and cloudless.

I found Nicholas sitting alone at the water's edge, staring across the sea. He was so still that I hated to disturb him, but I didn't want him to think I'd left too.

I remember how much I admired him in Cologne. I know I don't feel that way anymore. Maybe I was a little foolish then. In turn I've looked up to him and trusted him and doubted him, but until now I'd never felt sorry for him.

Before I could say anything, he turned around. "You're still here," he said in a flat voice. "I know many are gone."

I hunted for something helpful to say. "Not that many," I told him. "A lot of us are still with you. I'm still with you." But I was thinking of how many have dropped away, one by one, along our way. Maybe it's meant to be like that. Maybe only those with the strongest faith reach the end. But if that's true, I'm in trouble, because my faith comes and goes like gusts of wind.

I thought of how a voice had inspired Nicholas in the first place. He was so quiet now. Was the voice inside him silent now too? Was that it? Did Nicholas no longer know what to do? I wished hard that Otto were there so I could ask him what to do (which makes no sense at all, since I'm here only because I'm trying to find Otto).

So I asked Nicholas if it was possible we were looking in the wrong place. Feeble words, but after a moment he grabbed me by the shoulders, his eyes bright.

"I know what to do," he said. That was what I most wanted to hear! "We'll go to Rome," he added, nodding.

Rome? I felt a rising panic. Wasn't that away from the sea?

Nicholas talked on excitedly. We'd go see Pope Innocent himself, he'd point the way. I felt more and more troubled. Something told me this would take me further from my own goal, not closer. I wanted so much to be loyal to Nicholas, if not for the sake of his voice and his mission, then because I'm his friend. But I couldn't ruin my chances of finding Otto. So, I told Nicholas—about Otto, why I came to Cologne, everything.

He listened quietly until I had finished. After a silence he said I would have to choose for myself what path to follow now. By the distant look in his eyes, I knew that in his mind he was already on his own new path, to Rome.

It's night now, and I'm alone. They've all left, those who are still following Nicholas. I'm too tired to think anymore. Tomorrow I'll have to find my own answer.

25th day of August, 1212
Passage!

I don't have much time to tell what's happened. We may be off at any moment. I found him again—the man who'd been to the Holy Land—and this time I didn't let him get away so easily. He told me again to go home, which made me angry. He was acting like all the rest—the preachers, the Abbot—who say a boy can do nothing but

Welcome, Pilgrims, to Outremer

("BEYOND THE SEA," AS THE CHRISTIAN KINGDOM IN THE HOLY LAND IS KNOWN)

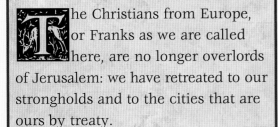

The Christians from Europe, or Franks as we are called there, are no longer overlords of Jerusalem: we have retreated to our strongholds and to the cities that are ours by treaty.

You'll find your fellow Europeans in Frankish cities, in castles garrisoned by permanent troops, in remote monasteries and churches where religious communities of monks and priests live, and in some small towns and villages (although most Franks prefer life in the hilltop cities that are protected and much cooler—villages are hot, old-fashioned places to live). ▶

wait to grow into a man. But I hid my anger and wouldn't leave him until he'd helped me.

At last he took me to a group of pilgrims traveling to the Holy Land, maybe just to get me off his hands. A truce is in place between Christian and Muslim (how can that be? there's so much I don't understand) and they're traveling on a merchant's ship to see Jerusalem once in this lifetime.

When I met them, they'd all paid for their passage and I was almost in despair. My gloomy warrior had vanished, and I had no more coins than would buy me a loaf of bread. I offered to work on board, but the ship's master said they had all the hands they needed and more passengers than they wanted. I lingered anyway, considering one scheme after another.

I saw the merchant who'd chartered the ship eyeing the medal hanging around my neck. I had never wondered if it was valuable or not, but when his eyes glinted I knew it was worth something. I hesitated only an instant before I sold it.

Did I betray Margarete? I'm not sure. I feel uneasy about it, but then I could look at it another way. This could be the very purpose it was meant to serve. She gave it to me to help me, didn't she?

We set sail as soon as the winds and weather are in our favor. Maybe now Margarete's saint will protect the merchant and his ship. I hope so.

Traveling to the Holy Land   2 of 2

Remember that we Franks are always outnumbered by the other people who live here: local Christians (often Greek-speaking), who belong to the Eastern Church, Jews, and Muslims of different cultures.

Don't worry if you get sick: you can expect better care here than at home. There are many excellent hospitals for sick pilgrims where the doctors have learned much from Arab medicine. In fact, the Franks who settle here always prefer to see a local doctor.

You'll also see Italian merchants come and go. Venice and Genoa are getting richer all the time by trading the goods they buy here back in Europe and from the constant traffic of paying pilgrims. (One witness estimated that 60,000 pilgrims came to the River Jordan in a single day!)

Venice

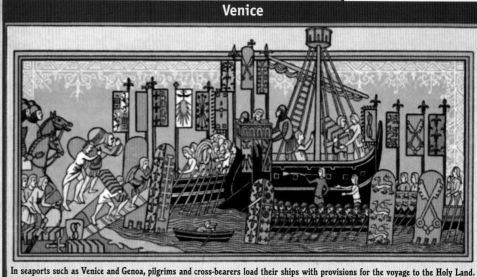

In seaports such as Venice and Genoa, pilgrims and cross-bearers load their ships with provisions for the voyage to the Holy Land.

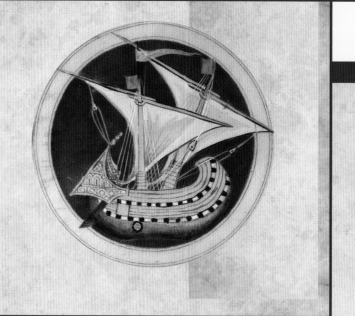

THE LAST BASTION

This sunny, hot island was a Greek colony in ancient times, and now most of the people here speak Greek and belong to the Eastern Church. It's been fought over many times, and has been ruled by both Muslim and Byzantine overlords. It was in the hands of a rebel governor when Richard the Lionheart conquered it while on his way to fight in the Holy Land. He had no interest in dealing with the unruly Cypriots and tried to sell it to the Templar knights, who did not want such rebellious subjects either. It is now ruled by a Frankish king, the 17-year-old son of a crusading family.

The island is the last bastion for Europeans on the way from Europe to more hostile lands. The ruling class is a small group of very wealthy French-speaking Europeans. Their subjects, both serfs and free, are very poor by comparison, and are mostly Greek, along with a handful of Armenians and Syrians. Newcomers to the island always remark on the startling inequality in wealth between the two groups, as well as the wonderful local wine.

2nd day of September, 1212
Island Kingdom

I don't know how to begin to describe this place; everything about it is so strange. It's an island, called <u>Cyprus</u>, and the Christians have built churches and strongholds here such as I've never seen.

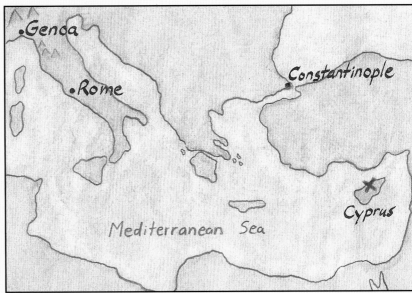

I'm told we are safe. The pilgrims won't stay long here; they're anxious to get to Jerusalem. I'll probably go with them, but I'm starting to wonder if Otto is even there. This land is much more complicated up close than it seemed from far away. There are many domains, and a ruler for each. Some are at peace, others in danger.

When we first walked toward the city from the port, something extraordinary happened. We passed many people on the dusty roads—monks, soldiers, merchants. Deeper in the city there was a maze of little streets with market stalls and people resting in the shade of stone walls. A voice made me jump. "Otto," it called. I looked around and saw a man waving to me. His face was sun-burned and he wore cloth wound about his head, but his breeches were like those we wear at home. "No, no, it's not him," his companion said, and they turned the corner. I ran after them, but the crowds blocked my way. By the time I rounded the wall, I couldn't find them.

After that, I asked everyone I met for news. No one had heard of the small band of volunteers I described leaving Westphalia two years ago. They're like drops that fell into a sea of men who come and go. French and German newcomers, people say, were in a coastal town when it fell to Muslim armies, and no one is known to have escaped. And there are rumors that last summer a ship carrying pilgrims back to an Italian port was wrecked.

I kept searching for that man in the street, but for all I can tell he vanished. Yesterday one of the pilgrims took me to see a man who claims he fled the doomed town before the Muslims over-ran it. I was exhausted from telling my story over and over, but I began it as always. As soon as I started talking, he interrupted to ask me where I was from. I told him about Wiesdorf, and he smiled and said he was from Aachen, not far from my village. (Once I would have called it far away, but not anymore!) I felt a throb in my chest when he spoke, but something else too: a hopeful feeling. It grew stronger when he told me he had come across a pack of youths—barely men, he said—from our homeland when he had been a day's walk from the Christian city of Acre. But nothing I said made him recall my brother.

Small crumbs of hope, I know, but they're all I have.

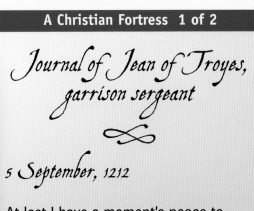

Journal of Jean of Troyes, garrison sergeant

5 September, 1212

At last I have a moment's peace to write these words to you tonight, Isabel my dear wife, though I know you may not read them for a long time.

Harsh words have been flying around here since a ship of cross-bearers arrived. Many of our country-men are shocked and upset when they arrive and see me (and others) dressed like the inhabitants of this land.

For a while I kept wearing the clothes from home that you made for me: my stockings and long-sleeved tunic with the short jacket overtop. But living in a desert country, we've learned to dress like the locals, for good reason! When we're at peace, ▶

11th day of September, 1212
A Choice

I left Cyprus with the pilgrims. We landed at Acre and headed south. Two days ago we took refuge in a Christian fortress, and now we are in more danger than ever. The Saracen army is camped in the distance; if I peek through the narrow window, I can see their torches in the dark. They came yesterday, and everyone expects an attack at first light. I'm told they've come for revenge. Christians barely off their ships, anxious to fight, were foolish enough to raid a village nearby, breaking a hard-won peace treaty. Now a battle is about to fall upon our heads.

It's getting late, and everyone is quiet, but no one is sleeping. One of the German archers here asked me how old I am. I confessed the truth. He thought it over, then told me I could probably slip out with the pilgrims before the enemy encircled us and head for a monastery not far from here, where we would probably be safe. Or I could take up a weapon and fight with the men.

I realize now that I have never really thought past finding Otto, never thought hard about what it would be like to fight, to use a weapon against someone. That's not Nicholas's plan; it never

Burnus

A Christian Fortress 2 of 2

we wear turbans to protect our heads from the sun, and stay cool in the long silk cloak they call a _burnus_. We go to public bathhouses regularly, and are much cleaner than when we lived at home. (I think I used to bathe a few times a year, if that much!) And we eat like the locals too; rich Franks even hire Egyptian cooks.

But don't be fooled. We may have taken on local customs, but Christian and Muslim do not mix, except in small ways during times of truce. It's a very delicate balance, one that's ruined whenever hotheads arrive from home, eager to battle the enemy at once, ignorant and disrespectful of the peace treaties in place, and shocked by our changed appearance and manners.

was. He wants to make Christians of the Muslims in the Holy Land. I wonder if he's on his way. Even if he is, it will be too late to help me.

Sneaking away to the monastery might keep me alive longer, and that could mean a handful more chances of finding Otto. But from what I've seen and heard, my hopes are growing slimmer. I'm not giving up, but every part of me resists running away and hiding. I want to do something useful. I complain about being treated like a child, so how can I run off when I'm given the chance to prove myself? And if I'm brave, if I help, they might let me stay, and then I can't help but find Otto one day. So I told the archer to count me among the men.

The pilgrims left hours ago. I've been given a sling (the one weapon I know how to use) and a narrow slit of a window to keep watch from. The men around me will ready the burning oil—Greek fire, they call it. There are hours to go before dawn. I'll lean back now and close my eyes, but I doubt I'll sleep.

Muslims in the Holy Land

Warm Greetings to You, My Fellow Syrians

You have asked me to describe these Franks who have invaded our shores, since as a diplomat I have traveled and lived among them in Jerusalem.

I tell you that I find their ways strange, often without honor, but now and then am surprised by their intelligence.

The Franks have no manly virtues except bravery. The knights are the only men who count among them. Once a decision has been pronounced by the knights, neither the king nor any other chief of the Franks can alter it. (Once I convinced them that in my land I am what they would call a knight, they treated me much better.) What they especially admire about a knight is his tallness and thinness!

The Franks who have been living here for a while and know our ways are much better than those who have more recently arrived. But they are an exception. It is always those who have just come to live in Frankish territory who show themselves more inhuman.

Once, when I was at prayer in Jerusalem, a Frank grabbed me roughly by the shoulders and insisted that I pray facing east. Templar knights standing nearby had to pull the man off, not once but twice. One of the knights explained that this was a newcomer who had never in his life seen anyone pray differently than himself.

I am at a loss for words to describe what the Franks call "medicine." A friend of mine witnessed the treatments of a Frankish doctor, who told a wounded soldier to sever his own leg, and who tried to cure a woman's madness by shaving her head and then, when that failed, cutting the shape of a cross on it. Unbelievable!

Their justice is not much better. A Frankish man said he had been falsely accused of guiding Muslim thieves into a Frankish village. He asked to face his accuser. The king of the Franks told the ruler of the robbed village to bring someone to duel him. The ruler chose the burly village blacksmith, and the accused man fared badly. This is justice?

Usamah Ibn Munqidh

FRANKISH ARMOR AND WEAPONS

THE KNIGHT

Helm
(metal helmet)

Nowadays the knights wear cylinder-shaped helms that cover the whole face, with slits for the eyes and holes for breathing. To make sure his men recognize him, a knight attaches his personal symbol to the top of his helm or to his shield. (Richard the Lionheart's was, naturally, a lion.)

Hauberk

This coat of chain mail, made of linked metal rings, falls to the knees or lower. A knight wears padded cloth or leather clothes underneath to stop the chafing and to spread the impact of a blow that could break bones. ▶

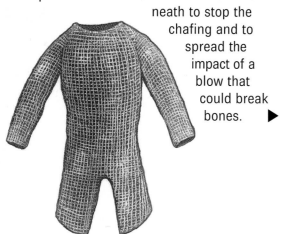

12th day of September, 1212
Siege

It's begun. They started at first light. Their battering ram is pounding our gates, and the walls shake with each strike. Arrows come in showers; some fly over the walls. We are all <u>ready for battle</u>. Whatever happens, I won't leave my post.

15th day of September, 1212
The End of the Path

There's a hole in my memory, or at least a space where everything blurs, as if I were looking through fog or water. Everything is clear up to a point. I remember the shouting men, the burning smell, and the panic when a flaming arrow fell onto hay. I stayed at my window, I hurled stone after stone. I remember someone calling, "They're over the south wall," and then pain shooting through my thigh.

Everyone was running past me. They must have been heading for the point where the wall had been breached. I tried to follow, but my leg crumbled beneath me and I fell. I saw unfamiliar faces and heard angry voices shouting in strange words. One stopped directly above me and barely glanced down before he stepped over

Shield

This is long and kite-shaped. Ones with flat tops are easier to see over.

Surcoat

Lately, knights have started covering their chain mail with a loose gown. It shields the chain mail from rain and the hot sun of the Holy Land. They probably got the idea from Muslim soldiers. (Enemy armies often steal good ideas from each other.) ▶

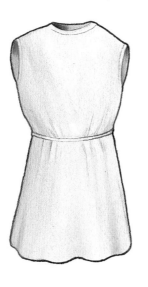

THE FOOT SOLDIER

He wears much less protection than the knights. Lucky ones have a thick felt garment covered by a mail shirt, a round metal hat, and a small round shield called a *buckler*. The farther back from danger you are, the less armor you get. A slinger has none at all, not even a hat. A soldier's armor might also depend on what he can afford. The poorest ones have only their weapon. ▶

WEAPONRY

Those <u>on horseback</u> rely on their *spear* or *lance* with a leaf-shaped head. Once it breaks in the crush of an advance, it's time to draw your *sword*.

Men on foot might have a *pick* (for piercing chain mail), a *mace*, or a *slingshot*. The peasants who set out with Peter the Hermit had no weapons, and no money to buy any. Farmers brought their hay forks, flails, and scythes; carpenters and wood-cutters brought their axes.

One of the most feared weapons is the *crossbow*: The soldier who fires this bow puts his foot in a stirrup, and bends over to attach the bowstring to a hook dangling from his waist. He spans the bow by straightening up, using the strength of his legs and back. Then he presses up the trigger to let fly the crossbow's bolt, a missile that's thicker and heavier than an arrow, and able to inflict much greater damage.

During an assault on a fortress, the enemy can use different siege engines to get through: the *tower* is pushed up against a wall so that soldiers can climb over, the *catapult* casts stones over the walls, and the *battering ram* smashes down the gates.

The defenders answer by hurling down stones, or boiling oil or water. Muslim defenders have been known to throw beehives at the Franks! The most deadly defense is *Greek fire*. Different mixes of ingredients (the recipes are closely guarded secrets) are heated or distilled into a brew that can be lit just before throwing or that bursts into flame on impact. Its fire is very hard to put out and will keep burning even on the surface of water. Some say vinegar will douse the flames, but don't count on it.

On Horseback

Military Brotherhoods

Newcomers to Outremer: In these lands, new orders of knights have sworn to band together to protect both pilgrims and territory. Here are the ones you should recognize on sight.

Hospitallers of St. John of Jerusalem (Knights of St. John)

You'll know them by the white, pointed cross they wear. The hospitallers started out running hospitals for pilgrims. Later they took on a military role as well. Their order, like many others, is divided into three kinds of brethren: knights, sergeants, and priests. ▶

my body and kept going. (Did he think I was dead, or just too young to worry about?)

I knew the fortress was burning, and that I had to move, but I could only drag myself along the ground. Another man halted above me. He wore robes the color of sand and a cloth wound about his head. I was sure I would not be so lucky twice, and I thought, There's no hope for me. But he spoke in words I understood. As he bent over me, his robe fell open and I saw a white tunic with a red cross on it. I dimly recognized it: the sign of one of the great <u>orders of knights</u>.

He frowned at the arrow in my leg, and when he glanced at my face he blinked in surprise and stared, as if he remembered me. But I had never seen him before in my life.

"Come with me," was all he said, but he was already heaving me up and over his shoulder. He carried me out of the stronghold, now almost abandoned, and draped me across a horse. I finally caught enough breath to ask where we were going.

"To the monastery," he said, and I groaned. He must have thought that was because of my leg, because he started telling me how they care for the sick there. They cured him when he himself was injured. I tried to protest, but it was no use.

It's after that ride across the sand that my memory dims. I think I was feverish. I remember finding every face frightening, and pulling with all my strength away from any hand that held me. I saw monks in brown robes, but to me they had demons' faces. I felt as if the fire had followed us and I was burning.

In the midst of it all, out of nowhere, I saw *his* face. Otto. Clearer and brighter than the others. I have died, I thought. I'm in paradise with Otto. It must be paradise, because that's where Otto would be.

Maybe hours or days passed like that, I have no idea, but I next remember lying awake in a cot, my throat so dry it pained me. It hurt to turn my head, but someone was coughing next to me and I couldn't help but look. There, on the cot beside mine, was Otto.

I had sometimes wondered, when I thought of how long he had been gone, if he would be changed, if I would know him right away. But I recognized him as I would my own hand or face, with a jolt that shot through me. I knew it was no dream, and that I was alive and that he was too.

Templar Knights

You'll recognize a Templar knight by his white cloak with a red cross. Their strongholds fly a banner that is half white, half black. After the Christians first conquered Jerusalem, some of the knights stayed to guard and serve the

Church established there. They decided to live like a religious order, vowing to be obedient, chaste, and poor. They called themselves the Chivalry of the Poor Knights of Christ, but most people know them by the name derived from their official home: the Temple of Solomon.

The Templars got the task of guarding the road from the sea to Jerusalem, and were soon fighting battles to defend the new Christian states, along with the Hospitallers. There are usually only 300 to 400 knights, so they take on cavalry, archers, and foot soldiers to make a permanent army. Templars have mighty fortresses in the Holy Land and enjoy privileges from their supporter, the Pope, which makes some rulers jealous. ▶

His eyes were shut and he was sleeping restlessly, tossing his head from side to side, muttering. I wanted to grab him by the shoulders and say his name and tell him everything, but I soon learned that things were not so simple. A monk (no demon!) appeared, and behind him stood the Templar knight who saved me.

"You're so alike," the knight said, pointing to me and Otto. He'd been sure, when he saw me, that we must be brothers. Otto had fought under him.

I tried to sit up, but my leg still hurt and I winced.

"That will take time to heal," the monk said, but added that it was not much compared to Otto's wounds. His arm was all but crushed. And, the monk tells me, his mind is wounded too.

3rd day of November, 1212
Looking Homeward

I spend all my time now with Otto. He didn't recognize me at first. I must look older than when he left—I saw my face reflected in the well and I think I have changed. He knows me now and we talk, at least for as long as the monks will let us before they make him rest. But I stay with him then as well. He has nightmares, and for a while after he wakes he's like someone groping through a fog,

Teutonic Knights

They're the ones in the white tunic with a black cross. Their sergeants, of less noble birth, wear a brown-black cloak. This order sprang up later than the Hospitallers and Templars. Starting out as a German hospital, they are now partly a charity serving pilgrims and partly a military force, and have built the castle of Montfort. Recruits are all German (Teutonic). To join, a young man must be over 14, unmarried, without debts or a master, and free of any physical blemish.

or else he's turned in on himself, looking at no one. Brother Simon says he hopes I will cure him. I hope so too.

Sometimes Otto's stories send chills through me. He never quite finishes them, and his mind wanders, but he tells me of battles, of ambushes, and once or twice he seemed to think he was there again and began shouting to someone. I think of how much I once wanted to hear about the adventures I imagined him having. Now I feel foolish, and a little ashamed.

I tell him about Wiesdorf—how tall Gisela has grown, what Father's taught me. None of it exciting or strange, to be sure, but he always sits up straighter and smiles while I talk.

I don't know if he will be able to use his right arm again, but he still has his left, and he has me. We'll sail home when the winter storms have passed. By then my leg will be strong. I used to think Otto would be the strong one when I found him; I'd counted on that, as if all I would have to do was put myself in his hands. Now I'll have to be the strong one for both of us, and I think I'm ready for that.

I'll take my brother home the way I came, unless I find a better path. So I may be able to keep my promise to Margarete after all, and go back for her, if she even wants to leave. Or she may have found a home where she is. Either way, I'll be able to show her my own miracle.

The Children's Crusade: Fact and Legend

Children who were lucky enough to return from the Children's Crusade—as it later came to be known—must have wondered what happened to their comrades. But they would have to wait many years for any news. Stories that did trickle homeward were often unreliable, and even now much of what happened remains a mystery.

This was a venture of common people rather than nobles, and so, fewer writers took the time to record its events. It was not even a Crusade in the usual sense: the mixture of children, youths, and adults was not an army, they carried no weapons, and they acted without the approval of the Pope or any ruler. It is hard to be completely sure which events in the so-called Children's Crusade really took place.

Some accounts were written by monks who witnessed the "infinite number" of children pass by. Chronicles mention more than one uprising of children and young people, and describe bands taking different routes toward the Holy Land. They record a movement in France led by

a boy named Stephen, who claimed to have a letter from Christ to be delivered to the French king, as well as one begun around Cologne by a boy named Nicholas.

The Chronicle of Cologne describes "a remarkable, indeed a more-than-remarkable affair" in the spring and early summer of 1212. Thousands of children, aged six years and up, were ignoring their parents' attempts to stop them, abandoning their plows, flocks, and herds, and rushing to take up the cross, as crusaders did. In groups of 20 to 100, they began to walk to Jerusalem. Another Cologne chronicle tells of French and German children taking part, and states that some wicked men joined just to steal the children's donations; one of them was caught.

One account from a monastery tells that many common people believed the children were inspired by God, and gave them food and help. They called the priests and others who discouraged the children envious "unbelievers." Some of the children were drawn away to join

(732)   THE CHILDREN'S CRUSADE.—Drawn by Gustave Doré.

the Crusade against the heretics led by Simon of Montfort. Many turned back at Mainz because it was too hot. Those who made it over the Alps and into Lombardy split apart. But the largest group, an estimated 7,000 at this point, arrived with Nicholas at Genoa.

It is recorded that Nicholas did lead a large group to Rome and that he met Pope Innocent III. One chronicler describes how the religious leader urged them all to go home, telling the boys that their vow to crusade was merely suspended, and that he would call upon them when they were men. According to the same chronicler, the Pope remarked, "These children put us to shame. They rush to redeem the Holy Land, while we sleep."

Other chronicles report that while many children perished or vanished during the journey, others were adopted by local families, some entered monasteries and convents, and still others were invited by the city of Genoa to stay and start new lives. Eighteenth-century Italian composer Antonio Vivaldi traced his ancestors back to one of these children. The children who braved the Alps a second time to return home trickled back alone or in pairs, and people who had fed them and cheered them on now shunned them because they had failed.

What happened to Nicholas is a mystery. Some chroniclers claimed that upon reaching adulthood, he joined the Pope's Fifth Crusade and then went home to Cologne.

As for the Christian Kingdom of Jerusalem, a year after Nicholas set out, Pope Innocent proclaimed the Fifth Crusade. The crusaders attacked Egypt, won a city there, and then lost it. During the next Crusade, Frederick II of Germany regained Jerusalem through negotiations with the Sultan of Egypt. Fifteen years later, the city fell to Khwarizmian Turks. The nobles of Europe became less willing to answer the call to raise armies for Crusades, and by 1291 the last major stronghold, at Acre, was conquered by the Sultan of Egypt and completely destroyed. The Franks in the remaining crusader centers retreated to the island of Cyprus and never won control of the Holy Land again.

Europe and the Holy Land at the time of the Children's Crusade (1212)

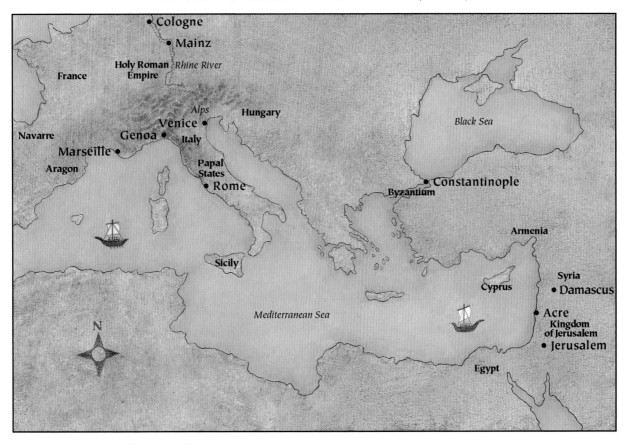

Probable route of the Children's Crusade ················
After Genoa, some children may have gone to Venice or Marseille.

Further Reading

Adams, Simon. *The Kingfisher Atlas of the Medieval World*. Boston: Kingfisher, 2007.

Davies, Kate, and Conrad Mason. *The Middle Ages*. History of Britain. London: Usborne Publishing Ltd., 2008.

Eastwood, Kay. *Medieval Society*. New York: Crabtree Publishing Co., 2004.

Elliott, Lynne. *Medieval Towns, Trade, and Travel*. New York: Crabtree Publishing Co., 2004.

Geyer, Flora. *Saladin: The Muslim Warrior Who Defended His People*. Washington, D.C.: National Geographic, 2006.

Hanawalt, Barbara A. *The Middle Ages: An Illustrated History*. New York: Oxford University Press, 1998.

Harpur, James. *Revelations: The Medieval World*. New York: Henry Holt and Co., 1995.

Jones, Rob Lloyd. *Crusaders*. London: Usborne Publishing Ltd., 2007.

Langley, Andrew. *Medieval Life*. London: Dorling Kindersley, 2002.

Rice, Melanie, Christopher Rice, and Christopher Gravett. *Crusades: The Struggle for the Holy Lands*. New York: Dorling Kindersley, 2001.

Image Credits

Sources

Allen, S.J., and Emilie Amt, eds. *The Crusades: A Reader.* Peterborough, Ontario: Broadview Press, 2003. (Medieval texts, including accounts of the Children's Crusade and the sack of Constantinople.)

Ashdown, Charles H. *Armour and Weapons in the Middle Ages.* 1925. Reprint, London: Harrap, 1975.

Benedict. *Rule of St. Benedict.* Edited by Timothy Fry. New York: Vintage Books, 1998.

Benvenisti, Meron. *The Crusaders in the Holy Land.* New York: Macmillan, 1972.

Delort, Robert. *Life in the Middle Ages.* Translated by Robert Allen. New York: Greenwich House, 1983.

Duby, Georges, ed. *A History of Private Life.* Vol. 2, *Revelations of the Medieval World.* Translated by Arthur Goldhammer. Cambridge, Massachusetts: Harvard University Press, 1988.

Friedman, John Block, ed. *Trade, Travel, and Exploration in the Middle Ages: An Encyclopedia.* New York: Garland, 2000.

Gies, Frances, and Joseph Gies. *Daily Life in Medieval Times.* New York: Black Dog & Leventhal Publishers, 1990.

Hallam, Elizabeth, ed. *Chronicles of the Crusades: Eyewitness Accounts of the Wars between Christianity and Islam.* Elizabeth, New Jersey: CLB, 1989.

Hoster, Joseph. *Guide to Cologne Cathedral.* Cologne: Greven, 1965.

Hunt, David. *Footprints in Cyprus: An Illustrated History.* London: Trigraph, 1990.

Jeep, John M., ed. *Medieval Germany: An Encyclopedia.* New York: Garland, 2001.

Madden, Thomas R., ed. *Crusades: The Illustrated History.* Ann Arbor: University of Michigan Press, 2004.

McKitterick, Rosamond, ed. *The Times Medieval World.* London: HarperCollins, 2003.

Norman, A. Vesey B. *The Medieval Soldier.* New York: Thomas Crowell, 1971.

Riley-Smith, Jonathan, ed. *The Atlas of the Crusades.* London: Times Books, 1990.

Riley-Smith, Jonathan, ed. *The Oxford Illustrated History of the Crusades.* Oxford: Oxford University Press, 2001.

Runciman, Sir Steven. *A History of the Crusades.* Vol. 3, *The Kingdom of Acre and the Later Crusades.* Cambridge: Cambridge University Press, 1987.

Stalcup, Brenda, ed. *The Crusades.* San Diego: Greenhaven Press, 2000.

Vauchez, André, Barrie Dobson, and Michael Lapidge, eds. *Encyclopedia of the Middle Ages.* 2 vols. Cambridge: James Clarke & Co., 2000.

Zacour, Norman P. "The Children's Crusade," in *A History of the Crusades.* Vol. 2, *The Later Crusades 1189–1311,* edited by Kenneth Setton, Robert Lee Wolf, and Harry W. Hazard, 325–342. Madison: University of Wisconsin Press, 1969. (For a discussion and evaluation of primary sources on the Children's Crusade.)

Glossary

Abbot: the head and religious leader of a community of monks

Christian: a follower of Christianity, the religion based on the life and teachings of Jesus Christ

Chronicle: a written record of events in the order they occur. During the Middle Ages most chronicles were kept by monks and educated people living at royal courts.

Crusades: military expeditions made by Christian Europeans from the 1000s to the 1200s, in which they attempted to oppose Muslim invasions and recover control of the Holy Land from Muslims

Heretic: a person whose beliefs have been rejected by Church authorities as false

Holy Land: an area on the eastern coast of the Mediterranean Sea, in what is now Israel and Palestine, considered sacred by Christians, Jews, and Muslims. Christians and Muslims fought over this territory during the Crusades.

Holy Roman Empire: from 800 to 1806, a territory ruled by an emperor, crowned by the Pope, with the goal of uniting Christianity under one rule. The size of the empire changed over time, and at different points included Germany, Austria, Switzerland, the Netherlands, northern Italy, and other areas.

Indulgence: pardon granted by the medieval Church that freed a person from doing penance or from punishment in the afterlife for sins committed in life

Knight: a man awarded an esteemed rank by his king or noble lord, and who fought for his lord in times of war

Mercenary: a soldier hired to serve in an army, in contrast to vassals, who gave their military service as part of the allegiance they owed a lord

Monastery: a community of monks who live together according to religious vows such as poverty and obedience

Monk: a member of a religious order who remains unmarried and lives apart from the rest of society in a community that prays, studies, and works together. Women who live together in such a community are known as nuns.

Muslim: a follower of Islam, the religion founded by the prophet Muhammad in Arabia in the 600s

Pilgrim: a person who travels to a holy place as an act of religious faith

Pope: in the Middle Ages, the head of the Christian Church in Europe. Today the Pope is the spiritual leader of the Roman Catholic Church.

Relic: part of the body of, or an item that belonged to, a dead, revered person such as a saint

Saracen: medieval name for a Muslim or Arab person

Vassal: in medieval society, a person who was given the use of land in exchange for their allegiance to a noble

Note:
The incident in Hameln described on page 22, the basis for the legend of the Pied Piper, took place after the events of the Children's Crusade, in 1237.

70

Index to sidebar information and maps

Note: Only the factual parts of the book (not the fictional story of Hans) are indexed. Page numbers in italics refer to illustrations.

Acre (city), 9, *9*, 36, *55*, 66, *67*
Albigensians, 9, 29–30
Alexius (emperor of Byzantium), 9
armor, 58–59, *60*

Benedict of Nursia, Saint, 33, *34*
Bernard of Clairvaux, Saint, 11
buckler, *59*
burnus, *56*
Byzantium, 9, *9*, *36*, 53, *67*

Carcassonne (city), 30
Cathars, 9, 29
chain mail, *58*, 59, *60*
Children's Crusade, 18, 64–66, *64*, *65*
  probable route of, *67*
Chivalry of the Poor Knights of Christ. *See*
    Templar knights
Christianity. *See also* Crusades; monasteries
  division between east and west, 9, 52, 53
  map of, *9*
  relics, 15, 43, 70
  the three paths, 23
Cologne (city), *28*, *67*
  cathedral, 15, *15*
  Chronicle of, 21, 65
  Fair, 13
Constantinople (city), 9, *9*, 42–43, *43*, 53,
    67
cross-bearers. *See* pilgrims
crossbow, 60
Crusades. *See also* Children's Crusade;
    Christianity
  attack on a Christian city, 42–43
  background and timeline, 9
  declining interest in, 66
  definition of, 3, 29, 70
  Fifth Crusade, 66
  recruitment of participants in, 11, 18,
      21–22, 29–30
  in south of France, 29–30
Cyprus, 9, *9*, *53*, 53, *55*, 66, *67*

Egypt, 8, 9, 66, *67*

foot soldier, *59*
France, *4*, *9*, *36*, *67*
  heretics in, 9, 29–30

uprising of young people in, 64–65
Franks, definition of, 3, 51
Frederick II (king of Germany), 66

Genoa (city), *46*, 52, *53*, 65, 66, *67*
Greek fire, 60
Gregory VII (pope), 9
guilds, 5, 13

Hameln, "Pied Piper" of, 22, 70
hauberk, *58*
helm, *58*
Holy Land. *See* Jerusalem
Holy Roman Empire, *4*, 9, 35, *36*, *67*, 70
Hospitallers of St. John of Jerusalem, 61,
      61, 62, 63

Ibn Munqidh, Usamah (Arab historian), 57
Innocent III (pope), 29, 30, 35, *36*, 66

Jean de Brienne (king of Jerusalem), 36, *36*
Jerusalem, *9*, *36*, *55*, *67*
  battles for, 9, 66
  European Christians in, 51–52, 55–56, 57,
      66
  king of, 36
  knights in, 61–63
  pilgrimage to, 15

knights
  armor and weaponry of, 58–60
  definition of, 70
  orders of, 61, 62, 63
  role of, 23, 57
Knights of St. John. *See* Hospitallers of
    St. John of Jerusalem
knucklebones (game), 6

Mainz (city), *28*, *38*, 65, *67*
medieval life. *See* guilds; knights; knuckle-
      bones; monasteries; tradespeople
monasteries, 33–34, 70. *See also* Christianity
Muslims in Holy Land, 9, 52, 56, 57

Nicholas (leader of Children's Crusade), 18,
      65, 66

Otto IV (Holy Roman Emperor), 35, *36*
Outremer. *See* Jerusalem

"Parzival and the Grail" (legend), *6*
Peter the Hermit, 22, 60
Philip II (king of France), 36, *36*
pilgrims
  definition of, 3, 70
  motivation of, 15
  numbers of, 52

Rhine River, 13, *28*, *38*, *46*, *67*
Richard I (king of England), 8, 9, 36, 53, 58
Richard the Lionheart. *See* Richard I (king of
      England)
Rome, *9*, 35, *53*, 66, *67*

Saladin (sultan of Egypt), 8, 9
shield, 59, *59*, *60*
siege, *30*
  of Constantinople, 42
  led by Simon of Montfort, 30
  weaponry used in, 60
Simon of Montfort, 29, 29–30, 65
Stephen of Cloyes (leader of Children's
      Crusade), 64–65
surcoat, *59*

"taking up the cross." *See* Crusades
Templar knights, 53, 57, *62*, 63
Teutonic knights, *63*
tradespeople, 5

Urban II (pope), 9

Venice, 9, *9*, 13, 43, *46*, *52*, 52, *67*
Vivaldi, Antonio (composer), 66

weaponry, 59–60
Westphalia, dukedom of, *4*

We acknowledge the support of the Canada Council for the Arts, the Ontario Arts Council, and the Government of Canada through the Book Publishing Industry Development Program (BPIDP) for our publishing activities.

ONTARIO ARTS COUNCIL
CONSEIL DES ARTS DE L'ONTARIO

Cataloging in Publication

Scandiffio, Laura
     Crusades / by Laura Scandiffio ; art by John Mantha.

(Kids @ the crossroads)
Includes bibliographical references and index.
ISBN 978-1-55451-146-4 (pbk.).—ISBN 978-1-55451-147-1 (bound)

    1. Crusades—Juvenile fiction.
I. Mantha, John II. Title. III. Series: Kids @ the crossroads

PS8637.C25 C75 2009   jC813'.6   C2009-901563-3

Distributed in Canada by:
Firefly Books Ltd.
66 Leek Crescent
Richmond Hill, ON
L4B 1H1

Published in the U.S.A. by:
Annick Press (U.S.) Ltd.
Distributed in the U.S.A. by:
Firefly Books (U.S.) Inc.
P.O. Box 1338
Ellicott Station
Buffalo, NY 14205

Printed in China.

Visit us at: www.annickpress.com

Acknowledgements

I am grateful to editor David Wichman for his guidance and ideas, and to Dr. Bert Hall, Institute for the History and Philosophy of Science and Technology, University of Toronto, for reviewing the manuscript and offering suggestions. Many thanks also to Sandra Booth for her image research and to Sheryl Shapiro for her thoughtful design work.

To Claire, who loves stories of long ago
      —L.S.